Copyright 2013 by Nikki Sex

This book is protected under the copyright laws of the United States of America. Any reproduction or other unauthorized use of the material or artwork herein is prohibited. This book is a work of fiction. Names, characters, places, brands, media, and incidents are either the product of the author's imagination or are used fictitiously. All rights reserved.

Acknowledgements

To Michelle, my snarky, heavily medicated Goodreads fan who inspired this story.

Also to David and Lisa, an extremely enlightened and innovative couple. Reading erotic fiction changed their lives for the better. May they influence many other couples to be honest with each other and act out their fantasies. Everyone should enjoy married life as much as they do.

Table of Contents

Prologue	1
The Kindle Affair	9
Ominous Beginning	17
Kindle Separation Anxiety	25
Password Puzzle	31
Magic	36
Analysis	42
Fantasy	48
Friday Afternoon	57
The Plan	65
Date Night	73
Comfortable	80
Neglect	86
Dominating Wendy	91
Faking	100
Honesty	108
Something New	116
Spanking	122
Vibrator	133
Frank's Fantasy	141
Connection	150
Neanderthal	162
Aftermath	170
BBQ	181
Epilogue	190

Prologue

When Wendy met his dominant gaze, something almost physical passed between them: temptation, burning heat and raw lust.

His dark eyes glittered with hunger.

Wendy's breath caught. Blood rushed in her veins and heated need pooled low in her belly and between her legs. Her eyes widened when his nostrils flared.

Good Lord! Could he suddenly scent her?

Fast and unexpected, he grabbed both of Wendy's wrists, twisting them behind her back and pushing her up against the wall. Wendy struggled, but only for a moment. Taken by surprise, she swallowed nervously, her throat suddenly dry.

Arousal and anxiety warred for supremacy in her mind.

The tall man was commanding and demanding. He had that perfect edge of sexy and rough that could only add to her erotic thrill.

Oh God, he smells and feels so good, she thought as sensation overtook logic.

The man's large body pressed close against her from his thighs, his narrow hips and groin, to her breasts. He was big and warm and hard all over. Evidence of his interest prodded firmly against her stomach. Arms secured behind her back, Wendy was utterly off balance and slightly uncomfortable.

What Wendy Wants

So why the hell, am I so damn turned on?

Her body flared to life in response to his scent, his strength and his domineering behavior. Wendy's pulse pounded in her ears and she strained toward him. Wanton and needy, she ached for more.

"You just keep still, now," he ordered in that low, slow, Kentucky accent.

His deep voice rolled over her flesh while the feel of his potent male strength made her knees buckle. His heated breath caressed her skin carrying a sweet bite of Scotch.

Wendy was naked.

The U.S. Marshal was fully dressed in cowboy boots, blue jeans, a blue button down shirt and tie. Then there was that large wide-brimmed Stetson hat. His eyes drank her in and his powerful male energy overwhelmed her with a potent masculine force.

She felt vulnerable, yet strangely powerful, too. This strong dominant man wanted her.

God damn he looked fine.

He transferred her captured wrists that were behind her back into his left hand, then pulled his right hand out and flung off his hat. It sailed across the room and landed on the hotel bed.

What Wendy Wants

His attention moved to her lips, a flare of need in his eyes. Putting his face against her neck, the Marshal inhaled deeply. Then he nuzzled and kissed her exposed throat. The whiskers of his five o'clock shadow brushed against her, trailing heated fire.

"You smell so good... I might just eat you right up," he drawled, pressing one denim-clad thigh in between her legs. That hard male leg rocked against her, rubbing her tender cleft.

Wendy moaned as she struggled to absorb the spike of pleasure that rolled through her. It was just as well that the Marshall had a good hold of her because otherwise she would have sunk right to the floor at that point. She felt boneless after his seductive touch.

Melting, Wendy surrendered completely.

There was no need for choice or decision. This man had all the power and control, while she had none. Why did that send a joyous thrill of happiness through her? Captured, constrained, all Wendy could do was feel.

Yielding completely, a delicious sensation of freedom moved her.

Hand cupping her jaw, he pulled her face toward him. He held Wendy there for a moment, his shrewd brown eyes looking right through her.

What did he see, looking at her so intimately? Did he have any idea just how much he turned her on? How much she wanted him?

What Wendy Wants

"Spread your legs," he bit out the command, his voice harsh with lust.

Wendy complied instantly. The Marshal cupped and squeezed her ass, pulling her into him. He moved in between her thighs, notching his big cock against her sex and pressing hip to hip.

The man radiated heat.

Tilting his pelvis, he pushed against her most sensitive flesh. His buttocks clenched as he rocked just slightly. This seductive tease ratcheted her arousal, creating a warm, throbbing pulse below the waist.

"Oh, God," she whispered, mesmerized. *The only sound in the silence of the room was her whimpers and heavy breathing.*

The Marshal leaned forward that last small distance. The hand that cupped her jaw moved to her hair, his fingers running through it and then winding tight. When he bowed her head to the side, tension pulled her scalp in a sexy bite of pain.

This excruciating zing of sensation pushed her to the brink of sensual overload. It was as if the pleasure centers in her brain were sizzling with energy and close to melt down.

With her firmly possessed and in the exact position he wanted her, the Marshal's soft lips closed on hers.

Wendy gave a strangled moan from somewhere deep in the back of her throat. Wired, wet and totally aroused, she opened her mouth, accepting and welcoming that kiss. His large frame held her fast against the wall, the hard male thickness of his denim clad cock stroking the sensitive lips of her sex.

With his sensuous lips against her, he never lost control of her, or of himself. As much as she willingly stretched toward him, this was his kiss, exactly as he wanted it. His lips were soft and firm — creating a hungry spike of heated desire.

She yielded completely as his tongue slipped into her mouth. With determined intent he explored her from the inside. Wendy's tongue found his, and she cried out with the euphoric joy of it. As he plundered her mouth, she joined in as they licked and sucked each other.

The feel of his long, lean body against her, the smell of him, the way he thrust against her cleft and his possessive kiss was all too much.

Mind, body and soul, she was in carnal overload. She was captured, unable to move... and she wanted to move.

Wendy struggled, seeking shamelessly to thrust and grind herself against him. He'd claimed her, dominating her in a way that made her want to give him everything she had.

So many erotic sensations! They all combined to hold her and keep her right on the edge of orgasm.

As his kisses delved deeper they also grew rougher. Pulling her head to the side by the hair, he began to suck and bite the sensitive skin of her neck.

What Wendy Wants

Wendy gasped, her breathing ragged. His every touch sent echoes of pleasure to every intimate area of her body. It would take very little to climax.

"Oh God, please," she moaned.

His hand moved down to caress the underside of one breast, and then his palm smoothed over it, cupping her fully. Her pussy tightened. Frissons of awareness sparked through her heated flesh. Her erect nipples begged for more as he rolled and tugged. Wendy whimpered, straining toward him.

She was aching with desire. "Please, please!" she gasped.

He gazed at her with hard eyes, his lips firm as he ran his hand lower, across her stomach and toward her sex.

"What do you want?" he asked in a rough voice, his body taut with lust.

Wendy was so turned on that she knew that she would orgasm with barely a caress, as long as it was lower.

"Please," she pleaded. "I need more. Touch me."

"Say my name," he ordered firmly. "Say my name and I'll give you what you crave."

Breathless, she said, "Raylan. Raylan Givens!"

"Yes," he said lowering his rough fingers down to touch her clit. "I want to feel you come."

What Wendy Wants

BUZZ - BUZZ - BUZZ - BUZZ

Holy shit!

Wendy's alarm rang at 7:30am Wednesday morning, just at the best part of her erotic dream.

Damn, it had been so real. Why couldn't that alarm have buzzed a couple of minutes later? So close yet so far away.

Wendy had been watching the television drama, '*Justified*' last night, and for the love of God, that actor Timothy Olyphant was seriously hot. Was it any wonder he carried over into her dreams?

"You okay, sweetheart?" her husband Frank said, resting a comforting hand on her shoulder, further shocking her back to reality.

Wendy rolled over and looked at her husband. His soft brown eyes reflected his concern.

Frank was a tall man, about 6'2", brown-haired and ruggedly handsome. He was almost forty years old and like most men, the aging process only seemed to make him more attractive.

Frank was big and strong and Wendy loved him dearly. Their sex life had been passionate and perfect when they first married. At one time just the thought of him made her wet. So why they hell was it that he just didn't do it for her anymore?

What Wendy Wants

She cleared her throat. "Er...why do you ask?"

"You were talking in your sleep and kind of moaning."

Wendy felt her cheeks heat. "What did I say?"

"Nothing that I could understand. What were you dreaming?"

"I don't remember," she lied, relieved.

Whew! Wendy thought, *close call.*

She would have been embarrassed to have to explain. How could she tell him? Lots of things turned her on, but unfortunately her husband didn't.

Not anymore.

∽What Wendy Wants∾

The Kindle Affair

Wednesday morning Frank Hayward was running late for work. As a consequence when he picked up his Kindle in a rush and threw it into his briefcase, he had no idea that the Kindle he'd grabbed belonged to his wife, Wendy.

Unknown to Frank, his wife liked reading romance.

Not just romance, *erotic* romance.

Well, smut, actually.

Sexy, dirty, kinky, delicious and utterly sexually arousing, smut.

It was the kind of smut that would make anyone totally rethink their sex life. A steamy type of book that would make a woman wonder: *Just how many orgasms can I have before I pass out from sexual overload?*

Wendy was right in the middle of a steaming hot story that made her want to discover that exact number for herself.

How much in life depends on tiny, little day-to-day choices? Or in Frank's case, not even a choice? On an error? On one careless oversight, a tiny goof that every human being is capable of?

Neither Wendy nor Frank had any idea of the consequences of that one little mistake.

What Wendy Wants

~~~

"MOM! WHERE ARE YOU?" her little dude, Jeff, their youngest, screamed.

Wendy sighed. For a six year-old he had a mighty set of lungs. She could hear his screeching voice from all the way downstairs, even when she was sitting in an upstairs bathroom.

The sound of little pounding feet vibrated up the stairs, across the landing and coming to a stop in the hallway just outside her bathroom.

"Are you in there?" his childish voice travelled through the door.

"Yes, you little monster," Wendy growled, while sitting on the toilet with her Kindle in one hand.

She'd gotten her husband Frank fed, organized and out the door to work. She'd hoped to have a tiny bit of peace and maybe even read some of that juicy erotica that she'd gotten half-way through.

The bathroom was the safest place to be alone... usually.

"What are you doing?" Jeff said in a curious and slightly plaintive whine.

"I came in here to have a nap and then maybe play some piano," she said wryly. "But now, since I'm here, I thought I may as well go to the bathroom."

What Wendy Wants

There was a couple of long heavy beats of silence as Jeff processed her snarky sarcasm.

"No you're not," Jeff said." You're hiding in there reading again, aren't you?"

Busted, Wendy thought, realizing that she hadn't even gotten as far as turning her Kindle on. *That kid is too damn smart for his own good.*

"Go away, Jeff," she said, keeping a lid on her irritation. "I'll be out in a second."

Wendy put her Kindle down with a sigh, got up, flushed and began to wash her hands.

She looked in the mirror. Hazel eyes, shoulder length brown hair. Nice figure, a few extra pounds, but no biggie. Well, maybe more than a few extra pounds. Unless it was wishful thinking, those boobs of hers had gotten bigger after having children. It was one advantage of motherhood.

After three kids I still look good, she told herself. *But I'm only thirty-eight after all.*

Wendy's Kindle rested on the counter, beckoning her enticingly.

"I'll get back to you later," she told it after deciding to leave it where it was.

What Wendy Wants

The erotic romance she'd read a few days ago had been incomprehensible in some parts. It was a sexy BDSM story, but it had a lot of humiliation in it.

Women had been crawling on all fours on the floor, wearing collars with leashes and had acted like furniture so that men could use them as objects.

She couldn't understand that aspect of dominance and submission. What in the hell could be the attraction to that? Particularly when humiliation was nothing new for her.

Wendy regularly got on her hands and knees while trying to pick up junk under the couch or the dining table. Objectified daily, she often stood like a human coat rack, offering clothes and lunch boxes while getting the kids out the door for school. And as for a collar! Wendy had prescription reading glasses since year eight. She'd lost them so many times that she'd decided to keep them permanently tied on a string around her neck.

Collared indeed.

Besides, she was a mom with twin teenage boys and a six year old. It was *their* duty to regularly mortify her and make her feel like an idiot. She didn't need to read about humiliation in a book when she experienced it on a daily basis.

What Wendy Wants

Yet those other aspects of BDSM – the spankings and bondage, not to mention fantastic multiple orgasms... well. That was a different matter. Wendy *really* wanted to try all that. Who knew what might happen? Maybe her love life would reach a whole new level. God knows, the level it was at now was an all-time low.

The truth was she'd become seriously bored with sex. She could climax more easily alone and with her vibrator than she could with her husband, Frank.

Wendy had recently read an article by Daniel Bergner in the New York Times. He asserted that it is *women* and *not men* who get bored with monogamy.

Bergner said that women are far more likely to lose interest in sex with their partners. It seemed that spouse-weary women often simply avoid making love altogether. Apparently they frequently needed novelty to get them in the mood.

Now, just how could she explain all that to Frank?

Looking at herself in the mirror again, Wendy pouted her lips and struck a sexy pose. Her brows furrowed and she sighed.

As much as she adored her husband, she'd fallen in love with and married Mr. Vanilla. He'd only been with three women in his life – and she had been one of them.

What Wendy Wants

Frank *could be* inventive, but he hadn't been for some time. He also traveled out of town for work quite often, which didn't help.

My Kindle and my battery operated boyfriend are my best friends!

True, a large part of it was her fault. She just couldn't figure out how to broach the subject more than she had. Her hints had gone straight over Frank's head.

It was embarrassing. For a high IQ, successful forensic accountant with astute attention to detail, he sure was missing her cues.

When it came to sex or making love, her husband was oblivious.

She remembered her latest attempt to spice things up in bed. She'd said, "Honey, sometimes I think that you should pretend I'm your sex toy, like a little game. Wouldn't that be fun?"

"Hum? Oh. Of course," he'd said, hopping on top of her missionary style. "You know I love you and sex is the best game in town."

At the time Wendy thought she could almost hear a whoosh of wind as her latest hint flew right over his head.

Of course that rush of air could have been just her own disappointed sigh.

What Wendy Wants

The man was so damn big and so strong – he could really take control if he wanted to. But how could she get him to *want to* dominate her?

Raising her eyebrows up and down while looking at herself in the mirror, Wendy smirked.

No, she would just have to be bluntly truthful. Toughen up and be more *frank* to poor Frank. How would that conversation go? She could just imagine it.

How about, "Frank, can you grab my hands, hold them above my head and then slam me against a wall and fuck me hard?"

She shook her head, frowning. As much as she would like to say that to him, she just couldn't.

"Honey, er…are your palms twitching?" she said out loud to herself in the mirror. Her lips curled up into a big ironic half smile. Frank would *so never* get that.

She bit her lower lip and thought it over. Maybe something like: "Honey, can you spank me? I've always wanted to know what that feels like – it seems kind of sexy. It may be fun to be bossed around a bit in bed, or tied up, too. Can you go all alpha male and exert your will over me? Make me submit to your sexual pleasure?"

What Wendy Wants

Just how would Frank react to any of that? Would he *get it* then? Or would he be ashamed of her? Embarrassed? Or worse, disgusted?

Just once Wendy wished she had the nerve to *really* tell him what she wanted. Until then she would go along with the status quo.

Wendy loved her husband. They got on so well, why couldn't she just be happy with that? She didn't want to jeopardize the good relationship that they did have.

At least I have my Kindle, she thought. *And my vibrator!*

What Wendy Wants

Ominous Beginning

Wiping her hands on her brand new chevron-sculpted bathroom towel that she'd picked up on special from Pottery Barn, Wendy felt a greasy blob transferring itself to her fingers.

What the hell?

Taking a closer look, the sticky brown blob was obvious. Well crapola. The damn thing had peanut butter on it.

"Kids," she said with disgust. "And I have three of the little demon spawn. Just what had I been thinking?"

Inhaling a deep breath and muttering something about the Lord giving her strength, she exited the bathroom with the dirty towel in her hand.

Leaving her Kindle on the bathroom countertop, she walked down the stairs. There was still plenty of time to get the kids fed, dressed and off to school.

While the boys were eating breakfast a quart of milk mysteriously fell over on the kitchen table. Not one of her boys sitting around the table moved until every drop spilled.

What Wendy Wants

Spilt milk! Wendy mused. *Ha!* Well, that was okay. A veteran mother of thirteen years, experienced in frontline childhood warfare, she was well above crying over *that*.

Then the six-month old golden retriever, Stanley, managed to start tearing a foam ball apart in the living room when no one was looking. Her youngest, Jeff, thought that this was hilarious and joined in the fun, trying to take the ball away from piranha pup. Pieces of foam went everywhere.

Joy.

When the twins began bickering, Wendy reverted to her favorite mental mantra. It was the one she used regularly that prevented her from wrapping her hands around the throat of one or more of her offspring: *I love my kids, I love my kids.*

Whoever imagined that twins were always really close? Her two fought all the time. While not identical, they were similar in looks and in temperament. Equally matched; each was as stubborn as the other.

Once all three boys were all out the door on the way to the school bus, Wendy sighed blissfully.

Should she grab her Kindle, go straight to her bedroom and finish reading that sexy story? The main characters had hated each other for the first few chapters of the book. Then all that hostility they'd stored up had suddenly burst into sizzling passion.

What Wendy Wants

Wendy had left the novel just as the hero was going down on his newfound love interest. The heroine was tearing at the sheets, writhing with ecstasy as her sexy lover lashed her clit with his tongue.

Delicious!

Oh, yeah. That was a panty-melting scene for sure. Wendy felt certain that she and her vibrator were both going to enjoy it. Despite the rigorous morning distractions and the resulting tension in her head and neck, she knew she was moist just thinking about it.

A little quality time spent with her BOB was exactly what she needed. *Can I say stress relief?* she snickered.

Disciplining herself to take care of business before pleasure, she decided to tidy the kitchen, sort out the dog mess and to make a list of 'Things to do' today before she indulged. She had a parent teacher 'Meet and greet' to attend for a start. Once she figured out her day's chores, she could focus on more pleasurable things.

Bang. The sound of the front door slamming open was an unwelcome surprise.

"Did not!" Will shouted.

"Did too!" Anthony screamed back.

What Wendy Wants

Crap. She immediately recognized the dulcet tones of her twin boys entering the house while yelling at the top of their lungs. These delightful sounds could often be heard when it came to either of them taking out the trash, cleaning messy bedrooms, or in fact during any expected chore.

All three boys seemed to have yelling matches when they were stuck inside during school holidays because of rain, too. Due to Murphy's Law, cable T.V. usually had an outage as well. Such arguments echoed in the closed house, sounding particularly loud then.

This time it seemed that the teens got into a kicking and punching fight at the bus stop. Will came home refusing to go to school; Anthony and Jeff trailed behind. Everyone missed the school bus.

Sweet Lord in heaven, Wendy thought once she'd sorted it all out and talked down Will, her highly agitated son. This unfortunately took about a half an hour.

What was I thinking naming him Will? That was certainly was a misnomer. I should have named him 'Won't.'

Calm, calm, she thought while taking a deep, steadying breath.

Wendy finally managed to escort her brood to her car, so that she could take them to school and personally watch them walk through the school doors. Once there, they would all be someone else's problem for the day.

What Wendy Wants

After the twins argued over which of them got to sit in the front seat, Wendy made them both sit in the back. The three boys piled into the car.

The only hitch was when little dude tried to buckle his seatbelt up while *still wearing his backpack* on his back.

The seatbelt wouldn't fit of course, but that didn't stop him from trying.

"Jeff honey," she said. "You forgot to take your school backpack off." Her youngest could be sensitive, so Wendy carefully concealed her somewhat hysterical bubble of laughter.

"Hey genius," Will snarked at him. "You're sharp as a bowling ball, do you know that?"

"Mom," Anthony said with an intentionally straight face. "Was Jeff adopted?"

Jeff's face crumpled with shame once he'd realized what he'd done.

"Knock it off, you two," she scolded. "Don't tease your brother. We're all in a hurry and it was an honest mistake. It could happen to any self-respecting six year old, right?" she said meeting Jeff's gaze.

He nodded and while his eyes welled, the tears didn't come, *thank God.*

What Wendy Wants

With two older, relentlessly teasing twin brothers, why did their youngest have to be an overly sensitive child?

After this morning's Super Bowl clash of family entertainment, Wendy finally managed to start the car and drive her little tribe off to school.

Inside of her silver SUV the twin's tensions still bristled in the back seat. When the unmistakable sounds of battle began directly behind her, she immediately regretted telling Jeff to sit in the front.

Damn it all. I should have known to split the twins up.

Wendy deliberately ignored the snarling whispers, slaps and pinches coming from the back seat. Selective deafness was one of the many time-honored survival mechanisms of motherhood.

It was a short drive and her mantra helped. *I love my kids. I love my kids.*

Outside the car, it was quiet and peaceful. The leaves were all turning with fall colors of reds, oranges and yellows. It was awe-inspiringly beautiful. Wilderness scenery surrounded them like something out of Walt Disney's 'Bambi.'

Wendy concentrated on that instead. Colorado was a particularly gorgeous State.

What Wendy Wants

The Hayward family lived in the Broadmoor area of Colorado Springs with a fantastic view of Cheyenne Mountain. The kids all went to Cheyenne Public Schools; the twins in High School and Jeff in Elementary.

Wendy dropped Jeff off first and then the twins. "Now listen you two," she admonished her boys as they got out of the car. "I want you both to start acting more like adults."

"Yeah, right," Anthony snorted with a mocking eye roll.

Highly approving of this subtle put down, Will giggled and affectionately punched his twin on the shoulder as a brotherly gesture signaling 'good one.'

The two conspirators laughed together, all upsets forgotten. Things were normal once more – the twins in harmony with each other in order to gang up on their mom.

Crap. Wendy scowled. That Anthony. He always seemed to have a quick reply that made her frown and want to rethink whatever she'd just said. She had to admit that it was a little silly to tell them to 'act more like adults' when clearly they both were adolescents.

"Don't talk back to me," she churlishly told Anthony, needing to have the last word.

What Wendy Wants

Oh well, she thought as she drove off. *That wasn't very adult of me, was it?* Never mind. It was her job as a mom to warp the next generation, just as her mother had warped her.

On the way home Wendy wondered if her life was the poster child example of why all Moms should be medicated.

Heavily.

As she turned into her driveway she felt her burdens lighten and her face stretch into an irrepressible grin.

Forget the kitchen, the shopping and the family room puppy-foam-in-pieces mess.

Wendy planned to go inside, make a fresh cup coffee and read more erotic romance. She deserved to spoil herself for an hour or two as a reward for surviving such a rocky start to the day.

Little did Wendy know that the day that had started off so badly, was only going to get worse.

What Wendy Wants

Kindle Separation Anxiety

Wendy grabbed her Kindle, made a coffee and a piece of toast. Mentally and physically drained, she dropped down on her favorite recliner, unbuttoned her jeans and put her feet up.

Gallantly following her everywhere, Stanley, the retriever pup, was also exhausted from the morning's activities. The pup circled three times and dropped down at her feet with a soft little puppy grunt.

The thing about puppies was that they were a bit like a light switch, full 'on,' or full 'off.' Turning to 'off.'

Stanley conked out and sprawled across the carpet, looking a bit like road kill. He was just so damn cute.

A familiar flutter of anticipation ran through Wendy as she turned her Kindle on. This was *her* time. Treasured alone moments of naughty pleasure, where she could escape to dominant, alpha male fantasyland.

With euphoric bliss, Wendy read: "*...heretofore accrual accounting was used to measure performance and position of a company, recognizing economic events regardless of when cash transactions occur....*"

Her mind blanked with confusion. *Say what?*

What Wendy Wants

Wendy re-read the text. When she went to Kindle 'home' the truth hit her.

I have Frank's Kindle.

Frank has my Kindle.

Oh my fucking God! Think. Think. Wendy reflected wildly, jumping up and beginning to pace. *So what? I don't get to read today, BUT can my husband read my stuff?*

No, she decided with a shake of her head. Bless her children. They had forced her to put a password in place.

The twins were obsessed with trying to find out what books were on their mom's Kindle. They often attempted to break through Wendy's password, or sneak up on her while reading. They also pestered the hell out of her about it.

It was payback, she figured, because she *loved* to torment the twins.

That was one of the best things about having twin teenagers, or in fact as she liked to call them, 'twinagers.'

Embarrassing them was a delightful pastime. Could anything be more fun? Subtly or openly, teasing her teens simply made it all worthwhile.

What Wendy Wants

The twins had Kindles of their own and as a parent, Wendy had access to their accounts. To amuse herself she downloaded books for them both such as: "Why Mother Knows Best," and, "What a Difference a Mom Makes."

Because of the twins, Wendy had set an unbreakable password on her Kindle. No obvious date of birth or mother's maiden name for her. But could Frank figure out the code? Would he even want to?

Wendy's brows drew down in a frown. If her genius husband decided to crack her Kindle password he absolutely could, there was no question of that.

A fresh surge of, *'Oh my God, will he find out?'* adrenaline spiked through her with electric zeal.

The possibility made her squirm. What if Frank read her erotic favorites? Or checked out her highlighted quotes? Would he think she was a pervert?

For a moment she saw her furtive reading activity through his eyes and felt ashamed and guilty over her depravity.

What was wrong with her? Why was she reading all this dirty raunchy stuff anyway?

Wendy began to load the dishwasher while she thought it through.

Driven, obsessed and brutally focused; her husband Frank was brilliant. He honestly was. If the man decided to get into her Kindle for some reason, Wendy had no doubt that he would do just that.

But why would he want to? I should call him and tell him that I have his Kindle. But would that get his curiosity going? Start the ignition sequence to his naturally investigative brain?

Shit! Should I do something? Do nothing? What?

Wiping up the table and counters, Wendy finished tidying the kitchen while managing only slightly to calm down. This insane state of nervous paranoia would drive her mad. She had to *know*.

On impulse, she decided to call Frank. Leaning against the kitchen counter, Wendy pulled out her cell and dialed his work number.

He picked up on the first ring. "Holdsworth."

"Hi, hon," she said.

"Oh, hello, is everything alright? he asked. "Why are you calling?"

This was a very good point. Wendy rarely called him at work unless it was lunch time.

"Well," she said, making her voice as nonchalant as possible. "I just sat down to enjoy my latest story on my Kindle. When I opened it, I started reading something about accounting. So, it seems to me, Frank, that you must have my Kindle."

"Oh," he said. "Give me a minute."

Wendy heard his leather chair creak as he no doubt reached over to pull the ereader out of his briefcase.

"Yeah, I just turned it on and it says: 'Enter Passcode.' This must be yours. Sorry. I was running late this morning and must have grabbed it. Never mind, I'll bring it home tonight. I'll probably work through lunch and get home early."

"That would be nice," she said.

Wendy immediately went into distracting him with a tale of the morning's activities. They both laughed over how much could go wrong with three boys and a puppy in the house.

"Okay, well I just wanted to tell you, if you are looking for your Kindle, I have it," she said in a voice of forced composure.

"Alright, sweetheart, I love you," Frank said.

"Love you, too," Wendy said, and hung up.

Fuckfuckfuckfuck! she thought. *Now I not only have to live without being able to finish that book, I also have to wait and worry all day long that my mastermind husband might decide to get into my Kindle and find my smut. Fuck a damn duck!*

Password Puzzle

Frank

~~~

Frank sat thoughtfully gazing at his wife's ereader. Her Kindle continued to recommend to him that he 'Enter Passcode.'

Restless, he stood up and walked to the window. It was mid-October, quite a beautiful time of year when the deciduous trees were all turning red, orange and yellow. Frank had a large office to himself and a beautiful view of Pikes Peak with its elevation of over fourteen-thousand feet.

The Peak's treeless crest was already sprinkled with snow.

The sky, as usual, was deep, clear blue. Frank had read somewhere that Colorado Springs had blue skies over three hundred days per year. Of course with an elevation of over six thousand feet, a good mile above sea level, a large portion of those days were below freezing.

A Senior Forensic Accountant, Frank loved his job. Nothing interested him more than a good puzzle. Born and bred in New York, he'd started work there where he had easily and rapidly moved up to the top pay scale possible in his industry.

What Wendy Wants

Wendy was from Colorado Springs and her family lived here. Because of that, they'd decided to move to Colorado once she'd had the twins. It seemed the best place to raise children.

As an experienced auditor, accountant and investigator of legal and financial documents, he was hired to look into possible suspicion of fraudulent activity within a company; or hired to prevent fraudulent activities from occurring. He was always at least three weeks ahead on his work because to him, his job was *fun*.

Frank loved details. He *adored* the minutia of facts and the process of performing analysis. It was in his nature to be naturally curious.

Just now his attention was focused on that Kindle.

Why had Wendy called? he wondered. *Obviously, I was going to discover that I had her Kindle at lunchtime anyway.*

After a minute of contemplation regarding possibilities, he realized that there was only one explanation: Wendy had something on her Kindle that she didn't want him to read.

The idea of her wanting to keep a secret from him stirred his initially mild interest into a burning compulsion. Frank decided that he'd read it.

But first he had to break her password.

What Wendy Wants

Having made up his mind, he ran a hand through his thick brown hair and set to work. He tried all the obvious possibilities, family birthdays, pet names, street names. The list was fairly extensive, but truthfully, he was enjoying himself. With a pen and paper, Frank kept a careful record of each attempt.

After exhausting the most likely codes, he sat back in his chair, rubbed his chin and really thought about it.

If I was my wife, what password would I use?

Wendy had created this to prevent the twins from gaining access – not him. She wouldn't have thought of keeping him out at all.

His wife knew that he would never have considered looking into her Kindle.

It simply wouldn't have crossed his mind.

Until now.

For a moment his thoughts returned to fifteen years ago, to the day they first met. Frank had gone on a blind date with another couple, one of them was Donald, his best friend and the Best Man at their wedding, and Donald's girlfriend, Anne.

What Wendy Wants

Naturally built like a football lineman, Frank's physique hadn't changed. Lifting weights had made him super stocky and as a sporty, active person he easily maintained his muscular build.

Big was just the way his body wanted to go.

Frank enjoyed playing football and he'd been good at it, but his favorite game was baseball. That was why his nose listed slightly to the right. He'd missed a fly ball while facing a bright noonday sun. The damn thing had broken his nose.

Man it had hurt like nothing else, but even worse it had been embarrassing to drop a catch in front of a stadium full of spectators during the high school championship game.

The upshot was that he looked a bit rough-edged and daunting, like a bouncer or a boxer.

Back then Frank figured most girls were afraid of him and honestly, he'd been shy. When he met Wendy, while not precisely a virgin, he'd been fairly sexually naive.

Frank would never forget that first date.

They had gone off to a College kegger in Brooklyn. While it hadn't been love or even lust at first sight, there had been mutual mild interest.

What Wendy Wants

Wendy, feisty little thing that she was, certainly hadn't been frightened of him. Yet what really settled the evening was how similar their reactions were to the party. Neither drank much, neither danced much.

They were standing near a table of finger-foods, one on either side. From time to time they both had been distractedly eating various snacks. That was the first time they really *saw* each other.

What happened had been comical and ridiculous, yet also magical.

In truth, that one moment had changed his life.

What Wendy Wants

Magic

Frank

~~~

His mind went back to that time.

He and Wendy had each been mindlessly absorbed, concentrating on watching the outrageous shenanigans of the party. People were chugging beer, some girls had stripped down to their bras and panties while dancing, some people were smoking dope and others engaged in a chase with a young woman as the prize.

Frank had felt like an observer engaged in an anthropological study of 'College tribal mating rituals.' He and his date, both intensely captivated, had absently reached into that bowl at the same time.

When their hands touched they looked up and met each other's gaze.

Humor and awareness had hit Frank with the force of a sledgehammer directly to the chest.

Here they were, young, healthy and ready to party. But instead they each preferred to watch… and to eat Cheetos.

What Wendy Wants

Their eyes had locked, mutually twinkling with surprise, understanding and amusement. A moment later, in perfect concert, they'd both burst out laughing.

Their date had been a winner after that. From then on they had been inseparable.

Wendy — beautiful, unique and amazing, was still the only woman for him.

Socially he'd felt kind of backward until he fell in love with Wendy. She smoothed his awkward edges. She made him feel more confident and at ease around people, particularly when it came to the opposite sex.

From time to time during his marriage, other women had hit on him. Frank figured that he was perhaps attractive to the opposite sex now that he was more mature and self-assured. Or did some women prefer married men?

Each time a woman flirted, he'd been flattered, but also quite uncomfortable.

No matter who come on to him, he would *never* cheat. Infidelity was something he just didn't agree with. Married and faithful, or divorce — that's what he always figured. Lucky for him, such loyalty was easy in his case.

What Wendy Wants

No other woman could ever come close to his wife, Wendy.

Thoughtfully, he tapped in the passcode: 'Cheetos.'

His eyes widened and his heart kicked into a little stutter as her Kindle instantly opened.

Frank drew in a deep and satisfying breath. That first moment of intimate connection had been vitally important to both of them. It still gave him a sense of awe and wonder. Right here, knowing Wendy's password, was proof of that.

He read on her Kindle from where she'd been reading:

"Arms over your head, sweetheart," Kurt ordered, "and spread those legs."

He took his time, parting her with his fingers, enjoying the lush pink swell of her pussy and running his tongue along her slit to taste her sweet honey. To his delight, she was panting breathlessly, with the occasional broken cry from deep in her throat.

When he slid a finger into her, while licking her clit, she became louder, fisting the sheets and begging him to fuck her.

Ah, he thought, utterly satisfied. *My shameless woman, overpowered with lust.*

What Wendy Wants

She was such a wanton greedy girl. Kurt loved to see her that way, enslaved by desire. He took his time fingering her, moving in and out, enjoying making her squirm.

From time to time he took Carmen's clit right into his mouth, suckling and nursing it. He felt it inside him then, throbbing away like an athlete's heartbeat during a marathon.

Man, could Carmen make some noise, or what? He smiled and thought about how he needed earplugs once more.

Her ability to resist orgasm was still astonishing, although he did pull back when he felt her coming too close.

What the hell?

A timeless flash of both confusion and clarity assailed Frank.

It was like those rare moments while pursuing an accounting case. Nothing makes sense. Then, *bang!* All of a sudden one elusive factor resolves every aspect.

Frank experienced a profound micro-second in time, where thousands of tiny details all consolidated into one perfect truth.

Wendy wasn't sexually satisfied in their marital bed.

His wife needed more.

What Wendy Wants

Brows drawn down in a frown, Frank shoved a hand through his hair and carefully considered what he'd read on her Kindle.

When was the last time he'd gone down on her? He couldn't even remember. His mind flicked through mental images of past sensual memories.

The numerous times Wendy had subtly refused his sexual advances and her obvious irritability whenever he approached her for sex.

The way she almost 'gave in' to sex sometimes, rather than joyously jumping him as she had for the first few years of marriage.

Was his wife coming to a climax whenever he did? Had he noticed?

As he thought back he realized that he'd been so absorbed in his own dick that he honestly had no idea if *she* was getting off. Was he the kind of insensitive guy who simply assumed that the woman he adored was having as much fun during sex as he was?

What had Wendy said on the weekend when they'd finally managed to get together to make love?

He frowned as he tried to recall exactly: *Honey, sometimes I think that you should pretend I'm your sex toy, like a little game. Wouldn't that be fun?*

What Wendy Wants

Kicking himself, Frank shook his head in disbelief. *How could I have been so blind?* Well, he could see clearly now. More importantly he knew just what he was going to do about it.

His eyes narrowed with determination and he sat forward in his chair.

First, he needed to find out exactly what Wendy wanted.

Analysis

Frank

~~~

He hit Kindle 'home' to check out just what the name of this book was. It was apparently titled, *"Carmen's New York Romance,"* by Nikki Sex.

Nikki Sex? Good lord! Who would ever come up with an absurd pen name like that? These authors are apparently creative enough to write an entire novel, but then can't think up a realistic pseudonym?

Wendy had a Kindle collection she'd named, 'Erotic favorites.' He made a careful note of every one in order to download and read himself.

He was astonished when he found her highlighted notes – all twenty-seven pages of them. He wandered out to the company photocopier in order to make a printed record to scrutinize at his leisure.

Frank usually read non-fiction, noting thoughts and ideas that would help him in his work. What had Wendy been highlighting?

What Wendy Wants

He returned to his office and stapled the papers together. His black leather chair squeaked as he sat back and put his feet up on the desk. Frank took the stapled hardcopy of her notes and highlights and read:

"The fun for me, Elizabeth is in controlling you," he said. "I want you submissive to my desires, powerless, and hungry to let me do whatever I wish – to obey and do whatever I say."

And this one, too:

"It is true. I am a good lover, but that is not so difficult. It requires only that I pay attention, and watch and listen to a woman and her body."

Huh. Well that was good advice. The author hit the nail right on the head with that one. Frank had certainly not been paying attention *at all*. But that was going to change.

Dumbfounded by his wife's interests, he flicked through the little booklet of quotes.

Wendy had highlighted a ton of stuff from this Frenchman, André Chevalier. He seemed to be her idea of the ultimate lover. Also Kurt Nielsen, the guy in *'Carmen's New York Romance,'* and Mike Thompson from *'Karma.'*

Her highlighted quotes had been both eye-opening and face tightening.

What Wendy Wants

Frank knew nothing about BDSM which apparently involved a variety of erotic practices involving dominance and submission, role-playing and restraint.

He just didn't get it. Why did Wendy want this? And why would he want to do it? Yet he valued his wife, and in his little heart of hearts, he knew that he would do anything to make her happy. He also knew that whatever turned her on, would also turn him on. Why wouldn't it?

Getting Wendy hot and excited always revved him up.

Treating this project like any other, Frank disengaged every thought except his forceful curiosity combined with a dedicated attention to detail. Three hours disappeared before he'd made his analysis of what his wife wanted to try during sex:

Spanking 76%

Submitting 65%

Hair pulling 57%

Neck/ nape bite/ nuzzle 55%

Bondage 55%

Oral (giving) 51%

Oral (receiving) 46%

Blindfold 30%

Nipple biting / pinching/ clamps 30%

What Wendy Wants

Frank couldn't believe it.

Spanking? Really? Why would she want that? He wasn't even sure if he *could* smack her on the butt. Yet, if it turned her on?

For a long moment the image of Wendy lying over his lap with her naked ass exposed and squirming flashed through his mind. His dick twitched. That sharp spark of sexual interest made him smile.

It certainly had possibilities.

Anal play was in there, too, really low in percentile, thank God. He wasn't sure if he was up to that, but hell, if Wendy wanted it? Frank would never refuse her.

Later they would discuss it. But why hadn't she spoken to him about any of this?

Frowning and restless, he stood up with his hands in his pockets.

She tried to talk about it, stupid, he told himself. *You were just thick as a plank. And maybe the subject is a little embarrassing for her to talk about.*

Frank left his office to pour himself another coffee from the staff lounge.

"Hey, Frank," Maxine, another accountant said as he passed. "How are you?"

What Wendy Wants

"Fine, just fine," he replied without looking at her. He continued walking, absentmindedly giving one syllable replies to another co-worker's greeting.

His mind was elsewhere, totally absorbed on his new puzzle, the mystery of Wendy's unspoken desires.

Returning to his office, he sat down and studied the entire book that his wife was currently reading. Afterwards he carefully returned it to the exact page that she'd been on, so that she wouldn't know that he'd cracked her code.

As far as he could tell, the male protagonists that she was interested in seemed to give the heroine multiple orgasms before they got off. Well. That sounded like fun.

He read a quote from, *"Elizabeth's Bondage Boxed Set."*

A woman's mind is geared to fantasy, while a man is visually focused. That explained the number of romance books that sold. Not to mention the very few woman's magazines picturing naked men, verses racks and racks of naked women in men's magazines in the newsstands.

What was the saying? How did you turn on a man? Just turn up, preferably naked. But to turn on a woman? That was something else entirely, for desire began in a woman's mind.

What Wendy Wants

Desire begins in a woman's mind. Frank echoed the thought, awed. *I get an erection just seeing a naked woman, but my wife? What does Wendy want?*

What Wendy Wants

Fantasy

Frank

~~~

Wow. Was Wendy reading these erotic fantasies and secretly masturbating to this kind of stuff? Just like he often did with internet porn? Was she ashamed of her sexual needs and her secret yearnings?

That possibility blew his mind.

Frank was embarrassed about his habit of watching internet porn and consequently had never spoken to her about it. He'd never joined a porn site; he just looked at free stuff on a daily basis.

Jerking off in the shower every morning was another thing he regularly did that his wife didn't know about.

Wendy wouldn't mind, Frank was certain.

So why did he feel so uncomfortable about telling her? Why would he admit to her his self-pleasuring activities at all?

Except that he was keeping sexual secrets.

A quote from her fantasy Frenchman, André Chevalier, flashed into Frank's mind with sudden clarity.

What Wendy Wants

"*Deceit is a barrier to intimacy.*"

It made him wonder, *Just when did I begin having more sex with myself than with my wife?*

Had he been afraid of a knock back? Wendy was no longer as eager to make love – that was for sure. Maybe he hadn't wanted to disturb her with his constant, unreasonable lust. But was it unreasonable?

In his wife's damn stories, the protagonists masturbated in front of each other – and the women were *always* wet, willing and ready.

Damn stories.

Startled, Frank suddenly heard *that* unexpected thought echo in his head.

Consciously he was embracing this, yet that one condemnatory thought indicated a less-than-understanding attitude.

Was he actually jealous of Wendy's love affair fantasies with her books? Maybe because he'd rather that she have a physical love affair with him? In point of fact, could he be envious of her book boyfriends and her self-pleasuring?

The idea of her getting off on her own created a resentful spike of unreasonable anger to flash through him. Did Wendy use a vibrator?

What Wendy Wants

Easy going, Frank never lost his temper, yet just the idea of Wendy laying in their marital bed and masturbating pissed him right off.

Yes, he decided, completely taken aback. *I'm actually jealous. Would she be jealous of all the time I spend watching porn and jerking-off, too?*

Frank sincerely hoped so.

Wow. These were all such new and astonishing thoughts. Had he and his wife been pretending? Were *they both* being less than truthful about what they wanted in bed?

The idea shocked him.

If that was the case, after thirteen years of marriage and genuine mutual love, it seemed surprisingly easy to drift apart.

Frank shook his head. How had it happened?

The rest of the day he spent doing internet searches, figuring out all he could about BDSM because that was what Wendy wanted. He found one quote that he particularly liked:

"When you screw up, own it. When your slave screws up, you own it."

While Frank would never consider calling his wife a slave and he sincerely hoped that she didn't want him to, he did think this was a relevant concept. Frank knew he'd screwed up. His wife wasn't sexually satisfied and that could only be his fault and responsibility.

It was a mistake that he fully intended to fix.

Another favorite author of Wendy's was Joey W. Hill. Frank found an article from Ms. Hill called, "Ten Tips for bringing BDSM into your bedroom." In it she said, **"The psychology of BDSM is what it's all about. The illusion of being dominated sexually, of submitting utterly to your lover – that's the turn on."**

Hmmm, he thought. *Now this is something I can really work with.*

Was that what excited her? The idea of being totally commanded and controlled during sex? The common denominator to Wendy's interests did appear to be in the area of complete submission.

Now that Frank reflected on it, it wasn't giving a head job that Wendy had highlighted with her heroines. It was when the heroine was *on her knees* while going down on the dominant alpha male. That seemed to be what did it for her.

The heroine always seemed happy to swallow, too.

Would Wendy do that for him?

Although he'd never spoken to her about, ejaculating right down her throat had been a long term fantasy.

Frank began to harden at that thought. As it was now, Wendy went down on him pretty rarely, but if she did, he'd shot his load elsewhere.

The idea of dominating his wife suddenly became a lot more interesting, particularly as he remembered that 'Submission' was pretty high up among her areas of interest at 65%. She'd look great on her knees with her mouth wrapped around his cock.

Hmm. Some of her sexual desires just might mesh perfectly with his own.

Would Wendy yield to his fantasy? Would she like to kneel down and suck him off?

His breath caught and he shut his eyes, suddenly overwhelmed with the idea of her swallowing every drop as he climaxed.

If he thought he could get away with it, he'd sure enjoy commanding her to do so. Those book boyfriend Dom's did. The corner of his mouth lifted in a devious smile.

I bet that I can get away with it, he decided.

Frank had all day Thursday and Friday to learn and prepare. He decided that he would take a few of his wife's favorite highlighted books and create an entire scene, following exactly what the characters in those stories did.

What Wendy Wants

He didn't need to re-invent the wheel. He could just follow a script.

Taking out his cell phone, he called Wendy's sister, Dawn.

"Hello?" she answered on the third ring.

"Hi, Dawn, it's Frank here," he said.

"Hey, Frank, what's up?"

"Dawn,' he explained, getting right down to business. "I'd like to surprise your sister this Friday and take her out to dinner and dancing. I just want to spoil her a little. We can both dress up and have an evening together at the Broadmoor. Would you mind having our boys overnight?"

"Ohhhh!" Dawn loudly shrieked, in what he assumed was wholehearted female approval. Frank held the phone away from his ear until the screeching sound died a natural death.

"Frank, that's such a *wonderful* idea," Dawn gushed. "Wendy will love it. What's the occasion? Or is there one?"

"No real occasion," he said.

"Really?"

What Wendy Wants

Dawn said nothing more, but he knew that she was dying to know what was going on. Neither of them spoke while he took a moment to collect his thoughts.

Frank liked his sister-in-law. A taller, four years older, and much stouter version of Wendy, she'd always been good company and supportive.

Unfortunately, Samuel Morrow, Dawn's husband could be lousy company and astonishingly annoying. Actually, the self-important idiot was *really* annoying.

He and Wendy would visit or have them over more often, but it was difficult to deal with Samuel. The man was not only stuck up, he had an exaggerated sense of his own importance.

Early in their relationship, Frank had accidently shortened his name to 'Sam.' Samuel's face had reddened with self-righteous indignation to the point that Frank had been worried that the man would have a coronary.

"My name is *"Samuel,"* he'd immediately corrected Frank. "I'll thank you to remember that."

Frank's nose wrinkled in distaste. *Arrogant, superior, prick.*

What Wendy Wants

Dawn, on the other hand, was down to earth and great company. She and *Samuel* had two girls, one eight and one nine. The cousins attended the same school and got on well, which was a bonus.

Frank decided to tell her the truth. "We haven't had much alone time together. I realized today that Wendy deserves better," he admitted with a sigh, feeling a little ashamed of himself. "This Friday I want to spoil her. We'll make it a big night, with flowers and everything. But I need this to be our secret until then."

This disclosure produced a somewhat lesser screech of approval from his sister-in-law.

A fast learner, Frank grinned broadly while holding the phone away from his ear. He'd been prepared for Dawn's excessively loud endorsement of his plans.

Talking a bit more, they went over details of the surprise.

When Frank hung up, he was pleased with himself. He intended to rock Wendy's world. He wasn't sure how exactly, not yet. But by the time he read her Kindle favorites, he knew he'd have formulated a detailed plan.

He'd started this whole investigation with curiosity and trepidation.

Now he was excited in a way he hadn't been in a long, long time.

What Wendy Wants

His stomach clenched and his heart twisted. It felt just like that first date feeling, that nervous anticipation or performance anxiety.

'Fake it till you make it,' was his customary rule in such situations. He was going to be 'the Dom' and give the orders.

How difficult could it be after all?

Wendy Hayward, he thought. *This Friday night you are going to have your every sexual fantasy come true.*

Friday Afternoon

Frank

~~~

Wednesday evening Frank returned his wife's Kindle almost as an afterthought. Her relief had been obvious. Neither approached each other for sex Wednesday or Thursday night.

Wednesday, Thursday and Friday during the day, Frank spent as much time as possible engaged in erotic study.

Friday afternoon he jerked off. Twice! Once late in the day because he didn't want to be desperate – tonight was all about Wendy and satisfying her desires. The other time he masturbated just because all this sexual reading made him intensely horny.

How was it that he had never actually bothered to study such an important subject? Satisfying the woman they love should be *first* on any man's most important 'to-do' list. That was Frank's priority now.

He could readily understand why Wendy had highlighted so much that André Chevalier, the sexy Frenchman had said. Like this one:

"The woman's sex, it is a magical thing! So absorbing and beguiling! As I teased and touched you, I watched, oh, so intently

did I watch! For your tight, closed channel began to unlock its secrets and open slowly of its own accord.

Soon the outer lips of your pussy spread wide and your sex became thick and plump. As you became more aroused your clitoris began to swell, and then it revealed itself, stiff and turgid.

It is the way of your sex, do you see? During arousal a woman's cunt opens like the most magnificent flower, the slick channel, the empty hole – it begins to gape, to open wide and drip its honey, begging to be filled with cock. The enticing fragrance of this flower then perfumes the air, drawing a man toward the scent to smell, to touch and taste."

His fingers caressed her, mesmerizing her with his hands and his words. "It is the way of nature, ma chèrie," he said in a low voice, "for a man to caress the flower of your sex in order to open its petals.

When you began to open for me, this gave me such pleasure." He took a deep breath in, and said intently, "To have this power over you, Elizabeth. For your cunt to willingly open, to submit to me and to my cock, this is what pleases me most of all."

Frank felt his pulse quicken as he read. *Hot damn.*

What Wendy Wants

How was it that he'd never really noticed the physical signs of how a woman's body altered when they were turned-on? With all his focus upon pleasuring his wife, Frank realized that he needed to understand the definitive signs of arousal.

Masters and Johnson filled the gap.

The vagina becomes lubricated, he read, the heart rate increases and breathing quickens. These things Frank had already observed.

But he never knew that the vagina increased in length and width. If he'd been attentive he could have seen his wife's outer lips grow large with engorgement as it exposed her vaginal opening.

This must be the opening flower thing that André Chevalier talked about.

A woman's clitoris was like a penis. Aroused, it increased in size by filling with blood. How had he missed that? But he hadn't gone down on Wendy in ages, and hadn't noticed what he was actually doing when he had.

The nipples become erect too – something he *had* observed. But Frank had never realized that a woman's breasts also become engorged. Mounting sexual tension then causes muscular contractions in various parts of the body as well as a 'sex flush' on the skin.

What Wendy Wants

Frank studied numerous diagrams of female anatomy. He hadn't even been aware of a 'clitoral hood' on the clitoris. Apparently once a certain level of excitement has been reached, the clitoris retracts under the clitoral hood and becomes inaccessible to direct stimulation.

Huh. Well he and his tongue were going to personally check that out tonight.

Masters and Johnson confirmed what he read in his wife's erotica: continued stimulation can bring a woman to a second and third orgasm immediately following the first one. In fact they said that many women were capable of having many orgasms in quick succession.

In the novel, '*Karma,*' on Wendy's Kindle, André Chevalier spoke about some of the possibilities of what could turn a woman on. Frank planned to ask his wife why she'd highlighted that section. Was there something specifically relevant?

The heroine of that novel had *never* experienced an orgasm… poor thing. Surprisingly this was apparently not that unusual for a large number of women.

Shit. What a disturbing thought.

Chevalier explored what the heroine may find sexy saying:

"Knowing that your lover understands you, and you understand him is important. Meeting the eyes of your partner during love-making may be an example of this.

Many women crave the intimacy that comes from love and communication. Part of an orgasm for you may be achieved through making such an honest skin-to-skin, soul-to-soul connection.

Does watching an erotic DVD arouse you? Or reading an erotic book? Do you imagine your lover doing these acts with you? To you? To him? Which acts in particular stimulate you?

Does the idea of you arousing your partner excite you? Or perhaps wearing erotic apparel or displaying yourself for his pleasure? Do you enjoy seeing him climax? Many women reach fever pitch at the idea of their partner using their bodies until they achieve orgasm. With some, the sight, smell or taste of a man's cum will trigger climax.

Think of kissing and touching. Are you aroused when you touch, taste or smell the object of your desire? Or when he touches you?"

All of these were good questions. But what were Wendy's answers? Is this why she highlighted this section? Or was it because she was experiencing difficulty climaxing? When Frank finally managed to talk with her, these were some of the things he planned to discuss.

He suddenly remembered that scene from the movie *Tootsie* where the sweet young thing is having a heart-to-heart with 'Dorothy' (Dustin Hoffman in drag).

The woman tells Hoffman, "I want someone who will come up and say: "You know, I could lay a big line on you and we could do a lot of role-playing, but the simple truth is, that I find you very interesting and want to make love to you."

Later when Hoffman as a man does exactly that, the woman hurls her drink in his face and storms off.

It made Frank worry. Maybe all this stuff appealed to Wendy's *fantasy* but might not work in *reality*.

He knew that he was taking a huge risk here by laying every card he had on the table. It didn't matter. He'd reconciled himself to it, because their happiness together as a married couple was so important.

Besides, honestly communicating may well result in marital bliss and triumph. This could be the catalyst that made their future together better than ever.

He'd checked the internet and decided to visit 'The Crypt,' which proclaimed to be a popular store for 'sex, leather and adults.'

What Wendy Wants

The store was only an hour to Denver from Colorado Springs. Frank, already ahead on every project, didn't feel in the least bit guilty about taking time off from work to drive there. He was too well known locally and didn't want to be seen visiting a kink shop in his home town.

While the 'South Park' boys grew up near Colorado Springs, there were a number of evangelical organizations in the area that would condemn sexual deviance of any sort.

As he didn't frequent adult stores Frank was worried about the seedy, creepy image he had of them in his head. 'The Crypt,' to his relief was pretty tame. It was well-lit and welcoming, like any other place of business.

Frank had made a list of things to buy. Silk scarves and candles he obtained locally. From the Crypt, he got some sheepskin softened leather cuffs with 'under the bed' restraints and a We-Vibe 3 vibrator.

He honestly had no idea, did Wendy have a toy she pleasured herself with? And if she did, why didn't he know about it? Whether she had a vibrator or not, that one had been mentioned in one of her erotic favorites, so he got it.

He was persuaded to buy the most expensive blindfold by the sales woman.

What Wendy Wants

"Oh this is my favorite," she gushed. "The silk elastic band will fit snuggly against the head, while double-layer brocade silk sashes extend to form a bow to tighten the fit."

Frank also bought a flogger, kind of a soft mop and a paddle.

He'd no idea if they would use all these things, but he wasn't in a hurry to come back here. If all went well, maybe he and Wendy would come here together.

So far everything was going to plan.

I'm going to give Wendy a number of orgasms, before I even have one, Frank decided. *Tonight is all about her.*

He frowned suddenly as a heavy thrum of excitement and anxiety went through him.

Well, he thought. *If it doesn't work out at the very least they would have a good laugh about it all.*

What Wendy Wants

The Plan

Frank

~~~

He called Wendy on his hands free while driving. "Hi, hon," he said.

"How was your day?" Wendy asked. "Are you on the way home?"

"I had to go to Denver, but I'll be home in an hour," he said. "Is your sister there yet?"

"No, why? Is she supposed to be?"

"Dawn is taking the kids to her house tonight," Frank said. "She'll be there by 6pm. I'll be home by then. You need to get ready because it's Friday night and I'm taking you out for dinner and dancing. We're going to the Broadmoor. I've made reservations at the Penrose Room."

"Really?" Wendy said, delighted. "What's the occasion?"

"No particular occasion, just that I love my wife," Frank said. He was pleased to find how excited Wendy was at the prospect of an evening out.

What Wendy Wants

"You are so darn sweet. Just a minute." It was quiet for a moment. "Sorry. I had to go into our bedroom so that I can talk without little ears everywhere listening in."

"Good idea. So, how was your day?" he asked.

Wendy gave a long sigh. "Well, it was busy. I had a "Meet the Teacher" for the twins this afternoon. It went surprisingly well, actually. I also ran into the 'Broadmoor Moms' of the neighborhood. You know it's like a Stepford clique here, right?"

"So I've heard."

"I don't think these women know how to walk out of their houses without being perfectly made up. I figured that my concession was that instead of wearing sweat shorts and a snarky t-shirt, I actually put on a pair of khaki shorts. They still got the snarky saying t-shirt, though. I can only bend so far..."

Imagining eyebrows raised in shock, Frank chuckled. "Which t-shirt did you wear?"

"The one that says, *Thirteen years after birth, hospitals should be required to issue straitjackets.*' Personally I've never decided if the straitjacket should be for the kid or the parents."

"Oh, the parents for sure," Frank said.

What Wendy Wants

"Ha! Speak for yourself. I'd rather put the twinagers in straitjackets. Maybe that would keep them out of trouble."

"Doubtful, but I can see your point."

"Oh, yeah, I also had to hold myself back from bitch slapping one of the soccer moms who thanked everyone for their work on fundraising, especially those who 'have more time than others.' As if I have nothing to do, just because I don't work full time."

Frank laughed loudly. Wendy could always make him laugh.

"And last but not least, little dude had his last swim lesson today. I've had a hell of a time not ripping the teacher a new one, because she is *totally* ineffective."

"That bad?"

"Worse. If I had to sit one more day and watch her walk the beginner class across the shallow end while they turn their arms, instead of working with the kids on, oh, I don't know, putting their faces into the freaking water, I may just spontaneously combust."

"Never mind. Jeff's only six. He'll have a better teacher next year. How are the twins?"

What Wendy Wants

"Anthony and Will got into their usual punching and kicking fight in the family room this afternoon. Anthony called Will a *douche bag*, and Will called him a *pussy*."

"Uh oh," Frank said.

"I know," she said. "The joys of the public school system, right?"

"I hate to think of how you responded," he said. "Are they both still breathing?"

"I swear I didn't touch them…."

"Oh, shit, Wendy," Frank said with an edge of alarm in his voice. "What did you say to them?"

A wicked peel of laughter came through the phone.

"First," she said, "I ascertained that they knew what those words actually were. Then I said to Will, 'Oh, so that means *you* go into *him*?'

After a large intake of shocked breath, he began to laugh. "No! You didn't."

Frank knew that Wendy never pulled any punches, especially with the twins now that they were teens. She was forthright with the kids and couldn't stand child-speak like 'pee pee.'

What Wendy Wants

It drove her crazy when other parents did that. "C'mon folks," she was likely to say, "It's a penis!"

"How did the boys come back from that?" he asked.

Wendy giggled. "Anthony said, 'Mom, you *didn't* just go there, *did* you?' But I bet they'll hesitate the next time they decide to throw those kinds of words around, right?"

"My clever, ultra-tactful wife," Frank said. "Always so considered and restrained. Adult therapy will cost them thousands – especially for poor Anthony."

"That's not fair," Wendy protested. "I didn't mean to walk in on him."

"I know you didn't, hon," Frank reassured her. "I still think it's funny. Being a teenager is difficult and Anthony was just sensitive."

About mid-year Wendy had tapped on Anthony's bedroom door and walked in. Anthony had been standing in his closet doorway, buck naked.

Before Wendy could think to guard her tongue, she'd let loose with a screech of, "Oh. My. God! You have *pubic hair*!"

Anthony hadn't talked to her for days.

What Wendy Wants

"I'll see you soon," Wendy said. "I'm going to take a shower and dress up, baby. You wait until you see what I'm going to be wearing. We're going to have such a good time tonight."

"That's true," he growled. "I've been feeling exceptionally frisky, so you just think about that."

"Reeeally?" she said thoughtfully.

"Yes, really," Frank said. "Don't imagine that you are going to get out of it. If you feel a headache coming on, take an aspirin. I fully intend to ravish you, wench."

This comment surprised another laugh out of her. Lighthearted and happy, he laughed at her laughter.

"You're on, baby," Wendy said.

After goodbyes, Frank disconnected his Bluetooth connection and thought about the evening ahead.

A number of emotions ran through him, excitement, nerves and lust. After reading about sex for three days straight, he was pretty damn horny.

He remembered Wendy's highlighted quote by André Chevalier, the fictional Frenchman known as the 'woman-whisperer' in the Nikki Sex novels.

What Wendy Wants

"I am a good lover, but that is not so difficult. It requires only that I pay attention and watch and listen to a woman and her body."

Tonight, Frank was going to concentrate on his wife.

He intended to make Wendy climax and climax and climax again....just like in those books that she'd been reading.

She'd been a horny, insatiable little slut when they were first together. Life had taken over, subtly absorbing his thoughts and interfering until he'd almost forgotten how it had been.

Could they actually revisit that time together? That period in their past where they never got enough of each other?

If he paid attention and watched and listened, he hoped to make her come so many times that she may eventually pass out from excessive, synapsis frying pleasure. Was that even possible?

He smiled. *I don't know for sure, but I want to find out.*

Besides...he was her Dominant for the night. It was up to him how many orgasms she had.

He'd memorized a number of Dom commands as per Kurt Nielsen the guy in *'Carmen's New York Romance,'* as well as André

What Wendy Wants

Chevalier in, *'Karma,'* and the ridiculously over-the-top sex scenes of *'Kink.'*

Frank had a step-by-step program planned. Wendy was going to be off balance and busy all night long.

Grinning all the way home, Frank's jaw felt sore from smiling. Whatever happened tonight, they were both going to have some serious *fun.*

~~~

Wendy hung up the phone with a thrill of exhilaration running through her.

Perfect, she decided, her jaw tight with resolve. *I'm going to dress up and even wear the garter belt and stockings I bought to surprise Frank. Tonight when we have sex, I am going to tell him what I want. By God I'm going to be honest and brave and somehow make him understand.*

What Wendy Wants

Date Night

Frank

~~~

The Broadmoor luxury hotel and resort was *the* place to go in Colorado Springs. It had seven hundred rooms, eighteen restaurants and cafes, three golf courses, tennis courts and a world-class spa.

The Penrose Room was the only Five-Diamond dining in all of Colorado. A popular conference destination for business and government officials, it was often fully booked.

When Frank got home he kissed his wife, surprising her with two-dozen red roses. Her response was more than he expected. Her entire face lit up, her eyes glittering with astonishment and honest joy.

After focusing on the art of seduction for the last three days, he was geared toward really noticing his wife and her reactions.

When had he last brought her flowers? He honestly couldn't recall.

"They're wonderful honey," she said as she bent her nose to them, breathing them in while she placed them in a vase. "So beautiful. But what brought this on?" Her eyes narrowed. "Are you feeling guilty or something?"

What Wendy Wants

"Maybe I am," he said. "Or maybe I've just realized how lucky I am to have you as my wife."

She laughed and brushed this praise off, but he could tell that he'd made her happy.

He showered, used a bit of his pricy sandalwood cologne and dressing in a tux. Women responded well to scent, he'd read. Frank had intended to shave, too, with his moderate five o'clock shadow, but Wendy stopped him.

"Don't shave," she said, cupping his face in her hand as she swept by him in the bathroom. Head up and hips swinging, she gave him a saucy wink and said, "I like a bit of stubble."

"Is that right?" he murmured, unable to take his eyes off her.

That dress Wendy was wearing was super sexy and the way she strutted in those three inch heels made his gut tighten. What the hell?

Were his elevated sexual vibes transferring to her?

Clearly his wife was on board with his preparations for an evening of seduction and mind-blowing sex.

Wendy had left her hair down, but had put an enticing wave in it. Frank wanted to see that silky mane of hers fanned out on a pillow as he fucked her, or perhaps hanging over her breasts while she was on her knees.

When he imagined those delicious red lips of hers wrapped around his cock he soon found that he had to adjust himself in his pants. Would Wendy be willing to drink his cum, when she'd never done so before?

Frank really wanted that.

He even had the command memorized from one of those books, the words to say when he came in her mouth:

"Take it, take it all… and swallow every fucking drop."

Frank wasn't sure if he had to nerve to order it, but that was what he intended to say when he shot his semen right down her throat. He stared at her, entranced by her natural grace and beauty. The muscles of his jaw clenched and his balls tightened.

"What is it, Frank?" Wendy asked after pausing on the threshold of the bathroom doorway.

He found that he was hardly able to speak his throat felt so thick.

"The way you look tonight, sweetheart," he paused and shook his head. "I'll try to hold back, but I'm afraid that you might have trouble walking tomorrow."

What Wendy Wants

Wendy's eyes widened and her eyebrows rose up. "Frank!" she said, shocked. Yet there was a flush of pleasure from this statement, too.

Dressed and ready, Frank opened the car door.

With care he guided his wife into the car with one hand on her elbow and one down along her lower back. Wendy gracefully got into the passenger seat.

He'd read that of all the senses, touch was one of the most important for women. They loved the intimate feel of skin on skin as well as extended kissing and caressing all over, not just breasts and genitals.

Touch apparently helped a woman tune into sensation and turn off thoughts so that they could climax more easily.

Frank intended to have his hands, and lips and mouth on his wife all night long.

Wendy was wearing a classy red strapless evening dress that accentuated every one of her beautiful curves. A Versace shawl and three inch open-toed heels finished the outfit.

As it was October, they wouldn't be able to dance outside on the patio. The temperature this time of year often dropped below freezing when the sun went down.

What Wendy Wants

When Wendy drew her long, lovely legs inside the car he blinked in astonishment. What exactly was she wearing?

His eyes narrowed with concentration. Her stockings appeared to be sheer silk.

"Those aren't panty hose, are they?" he asked.

Her lips quirked up in a sultry smile and a mischievous wink. "If you're lucky, you'll find out later exactly what they are."

Holy shit. The image of his wife naked in high heels while wearing a garter belt almost made his eyes cross.

Frank cleared his throat. "Keep teasing me like that and you won't be making it to the restaurant," he growled. "I might just do you in the car right now."

Wendy giggled happily at his warning and the sound of it made his heart soar.

Shutting the car door, he went around to the driver's side and got in.

It was a short drive to the Broadmoor. Frank listened as his wife told him stories of her day. He put a hiatus on his efforts at seduction while they laughed and chatted amicably together. He smiled, at ease and happy.

What Wendy Wants

Frank could be himself with his wife. They were comfortable and familiar with each other because they had always been good friends.

When their waiter escorted them to their table, he waved the man off when he attempted to pull out a chair for Wendy.

With a fleeting look of confusion and then a smile of understanding, the waiter nodded and left.

Frank wanted to seat his wife himself.

This was a night of seduction. All of his focus was going toward giving joy and pleasure to his beautiful, wonderful wife.

As Wendy sat down, he ran a hand along her bare arm in the process. To his astonishment, she lowered her eyes, displaying darkened, curled eyelashes and gave him a shy smile. Was that because the waiter was watching?

After she was seated, Frank gently ran his fingers along her shoulder and under her hair, curling the palm of his hand under her silky locks and possessively wrapping his fingers around her nape.

Wendy shivered and flushed slightly in response. Were those goose bumps?

What Wendy Wants

Neck/ nape 55%, Frank thought feeling extraordinarily smug. *Definitely an erogenous zone. Demonstrating possession is an alpha-male trait. Just like in all those erotic stories she's been reading, this should really turn her on.*

~What Wendy Wants~

Comfortable

Frank

~~~

He intentionally sat beside Wendy, rather than across from her. This way he was close and could hold her hand, or touch her from time to time. Touching was right up there, when it came to foreplay.

Tonight he wanted to set her on fire.

They both ordered the Acapulco Shrimp Ceviche, a house special for the night, with a chilled white wine that tasted of pears and peaches.

'Silver Service' in The Penrose Room was impeccable even though the place was packed. The entire dinner they talked and laughed. Frank flirted outrageously, openly undressing her with his eyes, while imagining what he planned to do to her later.

His wife seemed uncertain under his intent and carnal gaze.

He took her hand, sensually stroking his thumb over her palm before pressing his lips to her wrist. Her chest rose with a sharp intake of air. While she brushed his romantic conduct off with a self-conscious laugh, he knew that he was arousing her.

What Wendy Wants

She was a little out of her element; he was intentionally putting her off balance. That was part of the plan. Wendy had to let go – she had to let him guide her. And his intended result? Frank smiled. Multiple orgasms.

Yet for him to take control, first she had to lose it.

When they finished the meal he asked, "Desert?"

"Not for me," she said.

He patted his stomach. "I agree." Frank flagged down his waiter and paid the bill. "Then let's go dancing, but first," he said, bringing his wine glass up for a toast. "To the most beautiful woman in this room," he said with complete sincerity, "my stunning and absolutely gorgeous wife."

Wendy's lips curved in an uncertain, almost introverted or maybe shy smile.

Why was that? Other than today, when was the last time he complimented her on her looks?

Had it been so long ago, that she didn't even know how to *react* to such generous praise?

Wendy is the most important person in my world, he realized while they both drank to his toast. *She deserves so much more.*

What Wendy Wants

Frank wanted to make up for his thoughtless disregard. Reaching for her hand, he brought her knuckles to his lips, giving them a soft caress and a sexy little nibble.

"I mean it, you know," he said quietly. "No other woman compares to you."

A playful smile swept over her face. She shook her head and cleared her throat. "If you're trying to put me in the mood, Frank," she murmured. "I'm here to tell you that it's working."

Yes! Desire begins in a woman's mind, he reminded himself.

Standing up, he moved behind her chair. He leaned over and said in a low voice, seductively whispering into her ear, "Tonight I'm not going to simply put you in the mood. I'm going to make you scream – over and over again."

Wendy's face reddened, but not with embarrassment. Frank watched that blush travel to her arms and neck.

Was this that the sexual flush that he'd read about? She opened her mouth and then closed it again. Had he actually made her speechless?

Wendy stood up on somewhat shaky legs and Frank draped her shawl around her.

What Wendy Wants

Placing his palm low on her back, he intentionally pressed his fingers against her buttocks while guiding her purposefully to the elevator. Was that a shiver of pleasure he saw roll through her? By, God, it was!

Wendy was a vital, sexual woman who longed for the thrill and excitement of seduction. How stupid had he been for not giving her what she wanted? Frank shook his head, astonished by just how much he'd been missing.

They went to the second floor ballroom where a live band was performing. The music was eclectic; Western, Swing, Retro and Big Band. The band was playing, *"Put Your Head on My Shoulder."*

It seemed a good place to start.

Frank pulled her to him, nuzzling into her neck and nipping an ear lobe. Once more she shivered in response.

"Frank! You're an animal!" she said with a giggle,

"You ain't seen nothing yet, baby," he said with a laugh.

His hands gathered her in as they swayed to the music. One hand trailed down to her buttock, tracing along her garter belt to where they held up her stockings. The place was packed, so no one would notice.

"You are so fucking sexy, Wendy," he said.

What Wendy Wants

Her sweet sigh was long and low. With her head against his chest, she relaxed into his arms. "You're not so bad yourself."

"You bought these stockings to surprise me?"

"Yes." She grinned up at him, a mischievous sparkle in her eyes. "Are you surprised?"

His lips firmed as he gave her a hungry look. Grabbing her buttocks he pulled her against him so that she could feel the thickness of his desire.

"Yes," he said huskily. "I'm flattered, surprised, excited and so hard for you right now that all I can think of is getting you home and fucking you senseless. You'll be wearing those stockings and stilettos and nothing else."

Wendy gave a breathless little gasp, a response that Frank was more than happy with.

He raised a finger to brush a lock of hair from her face while gazing into her hazel eyes. She was beautiful. He felt so close to her. This wasn't just sex, although sex was a part of it.

This was his Wendy, the woman he'd married and the only woman for him.

The mother of his children.

What Wendy Wants

The love of his life.

"I'm a lucky guy," he murmured, and pressed his lips against hers in a soft, chaste kiss. As they kissed, Frank wrapped his fingers in her hair, intentionally giving it a little tug.

Wendy made a soft sound of pleasure.

Somewhere in the back of his relentlessly logical mind, Frank thought, *hair pulling 57%.*

Frank and Wendy had taken ballroom dancing lessons and some swing. It had been months since they had danced.

Why was it that having children had interrupted their personal time together? It didn't need to be that way.

A depressed sort of lazy apathy had silently snuck into their marriage.

The problem was that neither of them had noticed. Why? Their life together lacked the intimacy they once had, but it was good. Was it too troublesome to alter the status quo?

Clearly they had both been 'comfortable' with the way things were.

But not anymore, Frank vowed.

Neglect

Frank

~~~

He couldn't believe it. *I've taken our relationship for granted.*

The clarity of that realization was as shocking as jumping naked into a mountain stream when winter snows were melting.

What Frank had discovered had been difficult – yet liberating. He was coming to understand that he could have lost Wendy in the long term. Their loving bond could have simply slipped away.

There was so much he had to tell her when the time was right.

Sensual adventures, pushing boundaries, discussing unfulfilled fantasies and complete honesty – that was where he intended to go with her now.

Their past had been great with the wonder of new found love, and the heady chemistry that came with such love. But if he had anything to do with it, their future could be even brighter.

Frank saw this moment as his chance to make his marriage better than ever. And why shouldn't it be that way?

What Wendy Wants

His chest felt tight when he looked at his wife.

Wendy was the best thing that had ever happened to him.

Confidently moving her around the floor, Frank enjoyed himself, well aware that his wife was enjoying herself, too.

He certainly took the lead when they danced. Would it be as easy to take a commanding lead while making love?

The music pounded when the band played, *"A Crazy Little thing Call Love."*

Full of wild energy Frank swung and pivoted, twirling his wife up in the air and all around the ballroom floor. Other dancers watched and clapped while he and Wendy grinned and laughed with the pure joy of it.

A strong man, Frank knew that his dancing skill was partially from a physics principle, really. Bigger and heavier, he had the greater mass and weight after all. Physically, Wendy was so easy to take charge of. When dancing together, he effortlessly moved her and placed her exactly as he wished.

He recalled the Robert Frost quote about how dancing is a 'vertical expression of a horizontal desire.'

What Wendy Wants

That was usually true, particularly right now. Tonight he planned to move and place his wife exactly as he wanted while he made love to her.

His cock jerked at the thought.

Their eyes met again and again and they laughed together, gracefully demonstrating their rock-and-roll swing expertise.

After so many lessons together, Frank was a fluid and self-assured dancer.

He leaned into Wendy, giving her a teasing circle of the hips, spinning her full three-sixty degrees and then pulling her back against him. His chest pushed into the pillow of her breasts, intentionally moving against them.

Her nipples were erect.

That was only fair as he was achingly erect himself.

Frank subtly and openly displayed his longing. To him, Wendy was the only person in the whole room, much less on the dance floor.

Eventually they came together for an unhurried gliding waltz with, *"The Way You Look Tonight."*

Frank took it in a measured pace, his hands leisurely roaming over her. Their bodies pressed together as they swayed back and forth, slowly, sensually, back and forth.

What Wendy Wants

The song ended with them in a full body embrace.

Frank's cock strained against her, hard as rock.

Pulling her even closer, he let his wife know just how much she he wanted her. He nuzzled her neck, breathing against her skin while pressing numerous soft kisses on her throat, behind her ear and across her cheek.

Wendy moaned, making soft sounds of pleasure, her body melting into his.

Lips tantalizingly close; Frank didn't kiss her on the mouth. Instead he rested his head against her forehead. Lingering there, his nose brushed hers as he breathed in her soft, womanly scent and the light fragrance she wore.

His arms were a tight band around her torso, hers around his neck. There was an electric current of awareness between them, a solid bond.

It was much more than just lust.

Frank knew that Wendy wanted to be kissed. That was good because he sure as hell wanted to kiss her. But once he got started he didn't want to stop. Slowly, gently, he cupped her face and pressed his lips against her with loving reverence.

"I love you, honey," Wendy said, her eyes shining.

What Wendy Wants

"Let's go home," he said gruffly.

~What Wendy Wants~

Dominating Wendy

Frank

~~~

"Stay," Frank said to his wife once they were inside their house. He put an authoritative bite in his voice, so that she understood: This was *not* a request – this was a command.

Wendy raised surprised, inquisitive eyebrows at him.

"I'll be right back," he said with a reassuring smile.

Frank ran up the stairs to their bedroom and got out his stash of stuff, preparing. He set out all the candles he'd bought and lit them. They gave the perfect kind of romantic, sexy light.

He surveyed the room one last time and then trotted down the stairs. His grin widened when he saw her.

Wendy hadn't moved.

In three quick strides, he strode purposefully toward her and tossed her over one shoulder.

"Frank!" Wendy shrieked, laughing. "What are you doing?"

What Wendy Wants

He swatted her on the backside and she gave him a satisfying yelp of astonishment. "I'm taking full advantage of *my* wife." He stressed the word 'my' letting her know that she belonged to him, just like any self-respecting alpha male would.

As he walked up the stairs, one hand moved to throw Wendy's dress up and over her back. With his free hand, he slapped her buttocks.

Shocked, Wendy gasped. "You are a bad, bad, man."

"You have no idea," he said.

The look and feel of Wendy's ass, outlined with the stockings and garter belt blew his mind. Frank gave a muttered oath at the sight, and she gave him a throaty giggle. Once they were in his bedroom he put her down against a wall.

Wendy's eyes widened as she took in all the candles. They illuminated the room, creating a dreamy shimmer while releasing a slightly vanilla scent.

"Oh, Frank," she whispered, her face bright with awe.

"I was going for romantic."

She smiled up at him. "It's beautiful. I *love* it."

"Good. Stay right there," he ordered, reaching around and unzipping her dress.

What Wendy Wants

Taking it by the hem he pulled it up and over her head in one fluid motion. She wore some sort of lacy red lingerie set, matching bra and panties with garters and a suspender belt to hold up her sheer black stockings.

"Holy hell," he said, entranced.

"You like?" she asked, putting a hand on her hips, tilting her head and raising a leg in a sexy, modelling pose.

"Are you kidding?" he said, his voice resonating with admiration. "You bought this lingerie for me?"

"For us, actually," she smirked.

Frank made no attempt to hide the raw hunger in his eyes. "I *love* it. You are the most smoking hot woman I've ever seen."

Wendy giggled yet there it was again, that kind of shy, doubtful look.

Didn't the woman believe him? Couldn't she see how fantastic and desirable she was? Frank knew that Wendy, like a lot of women, was hyper-critical of her body.

Well, he decided. He would take all those misgivings away.

For a long moment, he simply drank her in, noticing every sexy part of her from toe to head. When he came to sensuous lips he stopped. They mesmerized him. Right now he wanted to kiss her more than he wanted to take his next breath.

With his hands firmly resting upon her shoulders and without saying a single word, Frank's lips pressed against hers.

When he pulled her against him, Wendy's mouth opened invitingly, her breath was sweet and she was so, so soft.

The sound of her quiet sigh ratcheted his arousal.

Frank shifted one hand, putting it around her neck and jaw. He could feel her pulse beating under his palm. When their tongues met, raw need rushed through him, flooding his body in an erotic wave of heat.

The heady feminine taste, scent and feel of her besieged his senses.

He inhaled sharply when he heard a small, needy sound from deep in her throat.

Frank felt his heart pounded loudly in his chest. His cock pushed against her, throbbing with desire.

When he pulled back, Wendy took a moment for her eyes to open. When they did, she simply stared at him, just as he did at her. This was a joining, a bonding of intense connection. How long had it been since they had shared such a kiss together?

What Wendy Wants

"Oh… wow," she whispered.

"You can say that again," he growled.

Her sexy new bra unhooked from the front, so he unclipped it and it dropped to the floor, exposing her completely. He took a couple of steps back.

"I love your gorgeous tits," he said. "Now take those panties off, and make me want you while you do it."

Her face lit with shock. "Seriously?"

His lips firmed. "Do I look like I'm joking?"

She laughed and did a little strip tease, bending over to show him her ass, while slowly removing her panties, lifting one foot and then the other. Once they were off she threw them at him. With a dull plop they hit his chest.

He grinned widely, taking a long moment to drink her in. "Halleluiah and praise the Lord," he breathed in a tone of reverential awe. "That was fantastic."

Her eyes shining with delight, she snickered.

"You're a walking wet dream, do you know that? Move for me. I want to see my steaming hot wife strut around bare-ass naked in those sexy, 'fuck me' heels and stockings."

What Wendy Wants

Smiling, Wendy proudly circled him with her head up, shoulders back and hips swinging.

She was into it, playing the game.

The woman looked like a catwalk model, or perhaps a dancer up on stage, sauntering out to mount her pole in a raunchy men's club.

Damn. Frank really wanted to fuck her, yet he had to wait. He deliberately intended to follow the plan. Wendy was going to climax a number of times first.

"Come here," he finally ordered in a husky voice.

When she was within reach, he backed her up against the wall. His large hands grasped her wrists and held them above her head while Wendy gave an incoherent squeal of surprise.

"Frank, what are you doing?"

"Shush," he said. "No speaking unless I ask you something," he ordered roughly, grinding his hard cock against her, letting her know just what he was interested in. "I'm going to fuck you and I am going to do it exactly the way *I* want," he said in a low, confident voice.

Inhaling in a deep breath of surprise, Wendy's eyes widened. As her lungs filled, her gorgeous breasts rose up enticingly, just begging to be touched and sucked.

What Wendy Wants

With her wrists firmly captured above her head, Frank plundered her mouth, this time in a passionate, bruising kiss.

Her familiar taste caused need to burn low in his belly, cock and balls. Arms, shoulders, chest and hips, he pressed himself along her naked flesh. He devoured her, deep and demanding, letting her know how much he desired her.

"Ahhh," Wendy responded in a soft, sexy sigh. Her whole body strained toward him.

Frank slid from her mouth and lips, moving to her collar bone before running his tongue up along her throat and neck, languidly kissing and sucking. He let his hot breath tickle along her sensitive skin to the hollow behind her ear.

When he licked then bit her earlobe, Wendy gave a low, throaty groan.

Shifting her wrists to his left hand, Frank kept her arms high above her. This was to increase her sense of helplessness. What better way for her to embrace the passion that was locked within?

With him in charge, Wendy would be grateful to let go. He wanted to set her free of all thought, all inhibition, all decision… everything.

Surrounded by sensation, she would climax *hard*.

What Wendy Wants

Running his fingers firmly down her body, Frank continued the assault on her senses. His lips moved lower, nuzzling and licking her breasts. Wendy's lush pink nipples proudly poked out, already distended and hard for him.

"God, I love your breasts," he said, fondling them. "Do you like it when I play with your beautiful tits?" he asked, giving one a squeeze with his palm while lightly flicking her nipple with his thumb.

"Oh, yes, yes," she said breathlessly. "Frank, it's so good."

He gave her a dark chuckle, pleased to have pleased her. Of course anything that got her off would get him off anyway. His engorged dick ached. It was just as well he'd jerked himself off earlier or he would have blue balls by now.

"Tell me what you want," he murmured in an intentionally dark and seductive voice.

"Oh, shit Frank, I just want you to fuck me already. I'm so super horny. I swear to God I'll die if you don't put that big cock of yours inside me."

He chuckled. "You are a naughty little slut, aren't you?" he said happily. "And I have no intention of fucking you yet."

"Aw," she whined.

What Wendy Wants

Wendy's whimpering protest pleased him. He was supposed to be the Dom, so he got to say when and how she got off.

"Besides, I want to play with you for a while first."

What Wendy Wants

Faking

Frank

~~~

While the primal part of him took control, Frank still had a logical mind that he'd trained for years to constantly take in and register *data*.

Just now he was cataloging every sign of her arousal.

Were Wendy's breasts swollen? They should be. He concentrated on them, giving each nipple a hard suck. Teeth gently nipping just over the edge of pain, he then soothed and laved with his lips and tongue.

Nipple biting / pinching 30%.

Frank's fingers trailed along her flank, to her waist and stomach, teasing through her pubic hair and lightly circling her clit. Hyperaware of her, he watched for every tell-tale sign of arousal.

The little changes in breathing, the low sigh or catch in her breath. Her eyes darkening, pupils dilating with sexual greed and need.

"Do you want me to make you come?" he asked in a misleadingly mild voice that hid a mountain of raw need.

"Oh, please," she begged.

What Wendy Wants

Wendy made desperate little sounds from the back of her throat. The musky scent of her arousal perfumed the air. Frank's nostrils flared as a white hot current of lust ran through him.

Fucking hell. She was ready and willing and that knowledge made his groin ache.

"Spread those sweet, soft thighs of yours further apart," he ordered. "I want access to that tight pussy."

Wendy gasped and instantly complied.

Raunchy or erotic words often turned women on he'd read and he could see that now.

Frank moved his fingers in a feathering caress through her pubic hair, between her legs. Her soft skin felt like warm liquid silk. Delicately parting the folds of her sex, he was shocked when he toyed with her entry.

She was dripping and he'd only just begun.

Wow. There was proof.

Without doubt, arousal starts with what's in a woman's mind. In this case their entire evening could be considered hours of foreplay.

A tiny, whole-body shudder went through her when he touched her heated sex. His warm palm cupped her mound possessively and in an instant his entire hand became flooded as her most feminine flesh spasmed.

Christ on a crutch. How fucking wet is she?

"Oh, God," she breathed.

Frank wondered, could he make her climax already? She certainly seemed close.

"That's right, be a good girl and I'll give you what you crave," he said, remembering to use the kind of coarse dialog that she'd highlighted on her Kindle. This dominance thing was really working. Frank couldn't recall Wendy *ever* being this turned on.

Jesus, I want to fuck her so badly.

His aching erection hardened further making him feel almost savage with sexual need. While squeezing her mound in a proprietary grip he sucked her neck, biting it fiercely.

Wendy gasped.

He pulled away and looked into her big wide eyes. "I'm going to do all the things I've always wanted to do with you tonight, my gorgeous horny wife. So you just stay right there and *don't move* while I play with your pretty little cunt."

Stunned, her mouth dropped open and her breath caught.

What Wendy Wants

A strangled kind of noise came from her then, something Frank had never heard before. Or maybe it was a sound he'd heard, but had never actually *listened* for. At exactly the same time he felt her stomach flatten and tighten under his palm. Was that a pre-orgasmic pulse? A kind of internal contraction?

Hmmm. He'd used that nasty word 'cunt' and she'd loved it.

Well, well, well. Such a *bad girl*. Wendy was primed, ready and hot as hell.

Frank had so immersed himself in Wendy's erotic books for the last three days that now that he was actually dominating her, it seemed an easy, natural thing to do.

She wanted this dominant and submissive kind of sex and by God, he was going to give it to her.

Being a Dom he'd found was a mindset and an attitude.

Frank's wife *belonged to him*. She was *his*. He could do as he liked. What he wanted to do was play with her until she had a number of orgasms that totally blew her mind.

While greedily suckling a nipple, Frank guided his fingers in between her folds, stroking along her slit. When he pushed two fingers up deep inside of her, curling upwards towards her stomach she gasped. He felt for the rougher area where her G spot was.

"Frank, oh, God, Frank," she cried out as her slick channel convulsed and gushed.

Her muscles tightened around his fingers *hard*, pulling him in. *Hot damn.* Her feminine scent perfumed the air.

"Yeah, baby," he said in a husky voice. "I'm going to make you come, aren't I?"

"Yes, oh, yes, please," she whimpered, writhing and straining toward him.

Not yet, he thought. *Make her beg for it.*

Wendy made a low, keening sound. Kind of a constant, rhythmic, "uh, uh, uh, uh."

It surprised him. When was the last time his wife had made this much noise during sex?

Frank had her body trapped against the wall, but she still managed to move. Undulating against him, she twisted, she squirmed and her head thrashed back and forth. Her breathing was ragged – he could see the pulse pounding in her throat at the exact purplish, discolored place that he'd bit her.

Holy shit, did I just give her a hickey? The thought that he had, made him smile.

What Wendy Wants

He used the pad of his thumb to circle her clitoris, while finger fucking her empty pussy.

Wendy's response was explosive, her hips arching as she shamelessly humped his fingers. He was careful to tease *around* her clit, not touching it for fear that she would climax.

"That's right," he demanded in a harsh voice. "Fuck my hand, baby. Hump that needy little cunt of yours against me."

"God, yes," she called out.

Her pelvis curling into him, Wendy did as he ordered, her hips jerking. Shining with sweat, hotter than Hades, she strained toward him, desperate for his touch.

Frank's breath caught from the sight of her. He was so entranced that for a moment he forgot to breathe.

"Please, please," Wendy implored him, her tone desperate.

"Tell me what you want," he snapped.

"More, Frank," Wendy begged and sobbed, her body grinding and rubbing up against his hips, his hand and cock. "Please touch me. I need to come!"

Frank *loved* it. Who was this greedy, passionate woman in his arms?

What Wendy Wants

What a wanton little slut I married.

By squeezed her wrists above her head, Frank reminded her that she was bound to his pleasure, under his care… and his will. Pushing deep inside of her, his thumb pressed firmly against her clit, flicking and rubbing hard. At the same time he also sucked and bit her nipple.

"Come for me, Wendy," he growled the command that he'd learned from all her erotic books.

The physical restraint of her body, the sensations to her full breasts and between her legs, all uniting with his forceful command all were too much. The combination sent her wild, successfully pushing her over the edge.

Yes! Yes! Yessssss! she screamed.

Wendy responded as if she'd been electrocuted. Back arching, she hit an explosive peak. Toes curling, her face contorted, body convulsing, she bucked against him as she rode wave upon wave of absolute pleasure.

To Frank her orgasm seemed to go on and on forever.

During climax he'd read that the uterus, vagina and anus contract simultaneously at about one-second intervals. A small orgasm may consist of three to five contractions, a big one, ten to fifteen.

This was really a *biggie*.

What Wendy Wants

Enormous.

A monster, in fact.

Panting like a racehorse, her hips pistoned while her whole body shuddered.

As Wendy eventually began to fall from the crest, she breathlessly uttered his name as if it were the last line of a song, or perhaps a prayer.

In an astonished, yet partially detached scientific manner, while still hard as rock, Frank watched it all.

Jesus fucking Christ. Had she been hot for it, or what?

While coming, Wendy had been loud.

Really loud.

Somewhere in the back of his mind, he remembered that she'd been pretty noisy when they were first together, too.

Frank had to wonder, all of this time, had his wife been *faking* orgasms?

Honesty

Frank

~~~

He held his wife while she came down from her climax, stroking and soothing until she stopped trembling. In those few minutes, Frank's mind reeled.

They'd both missed out on so much. How could he have neglected the woman he loved?

Statistically he'd heard that other than issues with substance abuse or mental illness, couples generally divorce over matters concerning money or sex.

Financially they were secure, but he'd been ignorant that they had an issue with sex.

How had it come to this? As years went by, he and Wendy could've become a divorce statistic, too.

Their marriage was far too important to let anything come between them.

Frank studied his beautiful wife; she seemed much more precious to him that ever.

What Wendy Wants

He was still dressed in his tux, while she was naked. This was another symbol of his power over her. He read somewhere that this was a turn on for some women, so what the hell.

Every little bit helped.

Frank wanted to make Wendy come a couple more times before he fucked her, so he may as well remain dressed. Right after a woman had an orgasm, it was said that the next climax was easier to achieve.

André Chevalier had said, **"I have not met a woman who is incapable of multiple orgasms."**

Tonight he'd find out if this was true

Wendy looked up at him, having come back to herself. "Wow," she said in a dreamy tone of awe, wearing a somewhat goofy grin.

Frank felt like a million bucks.

All his reading and study was worth it just for that.

In high spirits, he gave her his most boyish grin. Then he swept her up into his arms, walking over to a padded, armless chair and sat down with her on his lap.

"Are you going to tell me what's gotten into you, Frank?" Wendy asked.

"Yes," he said. "I broke the password to your Kindle on Wednesday."

She flinched, stiffened and sat up straight with in an oh-shit-I've-been-caught-out panicked look. The poor woman paled as the blood drained from her face. Soon after, her complexion reddened with shock or perhaps embarrassment.

He just had to feel sorry for his wife.

Taking no apparent notice of her discomfort, he continued, "So all day Wednesday, Thursday and Friday I've been studying about dominance and submission as well as reading your favorite authors."

He wrapped his arms around her in a soothing hug and then patted and rubbed her back. Despite that recent climax, her body remained tense.

"There's a lot of stuff we need to talk about," he said. "But not just yet. Right now I'm going to just ask you a few questions. It may be difficult, but I need you to tell me the truth. Be brutally honest, okay, baby? I think it's important. Just answer my questions. Can you do that?

Wendy swallowed. "All right, but you have to be honest, too."

"Of course. Ready?"

"Okay."

What Wendy Wants

"Do you have a vibrator?"

Embarrassed, her cheeks pinked as she ducked her head into her hands. "Oh God, just shoot me now. Yes, yes, I not only have a vibrator, I use it," she answered.

Ha! I thought so, he mused. *What a secretive wife I have.*

"How often do you use it?"

After a long pause she whispered, "Almost every day."

This was a huge blow, but Frank continued. "It is a We-Vibe 3?"

Confusion crossed her face. "Um… no."

"Do you masturbate after or while reading those erotic stories?"

"Yes."

"How often do you fake orgasm when you're having sex with me?"

Wendy's face and neck went scarlet once more and she literally squirmed and looked away. "Not every time…but um, most of the time."

Really? Despite his intention to remain calm and collected, Frank couldn't prevent his immediate frown.

What Wendy Wants

Her answer took the wind out of what had been, up until then, smooth sailing. His mind churned with disagreeable thoughts. Instantly upset, his stomach churned, too.

Wendy, his wife and the love of his life had felt the need to resort to lying to him? She'd been faking pleasure?

Her admission made him feel like a complete asshole. A selfish, stupid asshole. He hadn't even *noticed*. Now what? What could he say? What should he ask her?

A long moment passed.

"Did you fake it last time we had sex?"

"Er… yes."

"And the time before that?" The accountant in him picked at her for a while, purposefully demanding details until she finally told him the whole truth.

"I'm sorry, Frank," she admitted, gazing up at him and meeting his eyes. "It's been like this for a long time. When we have sex I come sometimes, but it takes a ton of effort and concentration on my part. It's just that it's so much easier to climax on my own and with a vibrator than it is with you."

He managed to school his face into a composed expression, but *wow*.

The truth hurt.

Frank came to his senses after a dizzying moment of anger and shame.

This was the edge of an unpleasant abyss.

Their romantic night was bogging down in baggage and bullshit, but at least for now he knew how to get both of them beyond this.

He took in a steadying breath. "And do you fake it with your other lovers?" he asked with a threatening tone of voice while scowling theatrically.

"What? Other lovers?" Wendy protested loudly. "Frank, you know there's no one else but you!"

"Hah! Fickle woman," he growled. "Do I? Do I really? You've lied to me about climaxing, how do I know you're not lying to me about having other lovers in your bed all day? And even on weekends sometimes? Such a wife should be punished, don't you think?"

He watched her process this. She was clearly wondering, why he'd make such an accusation. It was the weekend comment that made the light of understanding reach her eyes.

What Wendy Wants

They were together every weekend.

Frank could see from the look on her face that Wendy finally *got it*.

His over-done tone of voice and absurd accusations, on top of his complaining that she was 'lying' to him was all a ploy in this game of dominance, submission and discipline.

Frank knew his wife.

The stubborn, feisty woman was nothing if not game.

"Well," Wendy rolled her eyes at him while getting into the spirit of things. "You're so right. I *have* been very naughty. Of course I should be punished. Ah… what did you have in mind?"

Frank narrowed his eyes to look at her: to really *see her*.

From everything he'd read of her interests, Wendy wanted all decision taken out of the sexual equation. That would set her mind free, making it easier for her to come.

The idea was so foreign to him. As a normal man, he *never* experienced any difficulty attaining release. It astonished him that his wife found that she had to concentrate and really work hard to reach orgasm.

It apparently wasn't difficult for her to climax when he ran the show.

What Wendy Wants

In the future he'd try to make sure that she came *first*, every single time they made love. *'Ladies first,'* was his new mantra. Like opening a door for her, it seemed only good manners for a man to allow a woman to go before him anyway.

He sat up straighter and gave Wendy an intentionally predatory gaze. "I'm going to give you a spanking."

She tensed. "You are?" she asked, with an uncertain expression on her face.

"Oh yeah," he confirmed. "I'm going to give it to you alright. I'm going to spank you so hard that you won't be able to sit down for a week."

What Wendy Wants

Something New

Frank

~~~

Frank's jaw tightened as Wendy shifted nervously.

"I think you'd *like* to be spanked, isn't that the case?"

He began running his fingers gently between her legs and through her swollen entry. It was a distraction, to keep them both on track for where the night was going.

She sighed and her flesh twitched in reaction as he touched her, caressing her clit in slow, lazy circles. Frank was beginning to discover that his wife was an incredibly sensual creature.

"Mm, yes," she said, placing a hand on his forearm to steady herself.

"Tell me what about getting spanked turns you on?"

Wendy frowned, bit her lip and looked away. "Oh, Frank, this is so embarrassing. I don't know. Pain improves climax it's said, not that I want a lot of pain. The idea of being naughty and being punished might be part of it. Or the fact of you holding me down? I honestly don't know. Maybe I'll hate it, but I do want to try it."

What Wendy Wants

There was more she wasn't saying and Frank kept at her until she finally gave in and confided, "It's just that I feel like a pervert for wanting to try this sort of stuff."

He wrapped his arms back around her in a soothing embrace. "You're not a pervert, Wendy. You're a beautiful woman who's curious about some things," he whispered behind her ear, his nose in her hair while nuzzling along her neck. She sighed, long and low.

"And you know what else?

"What?" she whispered.

"You're really bored with sex," he said.

"That's not true, honey," she protested. "You're a sweet lover, Frank."

He shushed her. "You don't want sweet."

She snorted, raising her eyebrows. A quick flash of humor lit her face. "Well, you know me. I'm going for mean and nasty."

He chuckled. "I've neglected my beautiful wife, but all that's going to change."

Wendy kissed his cheek. "Thank you," she said. "You're the best, hon."

He chuckled. "Well, don't thank me yet," he warned. "Let's see what you think after I spank you. The first bit is going to really hurt. I'm going to give you five really hard spanks as punishment. After that will be the sexy spanks for pleasure."

"Really? And what am I being punished for again?" she asked with a nervous frown between her brows.

"To remind you that you will never masturbate and climax without my approval," he said firmly, "and you will never again fake orgasm. When you sit down you will remember that *you are mine* and that you climax *with me* or not at all."

Frank was surprised by the intense way he was laying down the law. It hadn't been completely part of his plan just at this point. The spanking yes, but somehow in getting into all this stuff it was as if he was channeling Dom behavior.

He felt insulted that she'd been faking it. She'd been having sex without him while denying him the pleasure of her body.

"When you screw up, own it," the books advised him.

Ultimately, he was to blame.

And he'd been doing the exact same thing, masturbating without her, so this discipline was certainly a double standard.

But, Frank decided dryly, she was still the one who was going to get the spanking. Getting spanked was her turn-on. Giving one might just possibly be his. He'd soon find out.

"Any questions?" he asked.

Wendy shook her head.

"Oh, and you probably know all about safe words and stuff like that – better than I do. What do you want to use? Red, stop; yellow, wait; and green, all okay?"

"That'll work," she said.

"Good," he said, giving her and intentionally wicked smile. "I've been looking forward to this," he said, and strangely, it was true. All of his misgivings disappeared.

With one swift move, he had Wendy across his lap with her head down. Her beautiful buttocks presented themselves, such soft, white, round globes. His cock, already fully erect, instantly got harder.

"Spread those legs," he said.

With a quiver of nerves or lust or fright she instantly did so. He stroked between her folds, marveling at how much slick moisture her body produced when aroused. How long had it been since she'd been this wet for him?

What Wendy Wants

Frank slipped one finger up inside of her. Wendy's instant moan was low and throaty as her sodden pussy clenched around him.

Fuck! Is she ready to climax again already? he wondered.

"God damn you turn me on," he rasped and was forced to clear his throat. His voice sounded harsh to his own ears. "Do you remember your safe word?"

"Yes," she whispered.

"Good."

Frank began by warming her lower body up, rubbing and squeezing her buttocks with both hands. He massaged every part of her with firm, stimulating strokes. Apparently this would help prevent bruising.

He'd read all about how to deliver a spanking on FetLife.

A couple of days ago Frank set up a profile on FetLife, a social internet network run by kinksters for people interested in BDSM, fetishism and kink. The site had freaked him out a bit at first, because it clearly catered to every extreme.

He spent some time reading message boards, reviewing profiles and talking to people in chat rooms. People on the site recognized that he was a newbie. They'd bent over backwards to assist him, offering advice and suggestions.

Until now, Frank had been uncertain if he would be able to spank his wife. But seeing her like this, ass in the air, ready for him, while knowing that she was wet and hot for it, took his every doubt and reservation away.

God damn it, I'm going to make those white cheeks of hers pink, he decided.

What Wendy Wants

Spanking

Wendy

~~~

Frank's going to spank me! Frank's going to spank me!

Wendy's mind echoed with that thought as Frank gently, yet with definite purpose, stroked and massaged her buttocks.

Her head was upside down, a lock of hair over her face. The room looked strange from this position.

Wendy was draped over her husband's lap, hugging his legs. She knew that she wasn't small, but her husband was such a big guy, he easily dwarfed her.

The way he arranged her across his lap was a real turn on. In this position she felt so vulnerable and available for anything he wanted. What he wanted was to spank her.

Her stomach flip-flopped as an electric spike of erotic sensation rolled through her with *that* thought.

Frank had broken into her Kindle and discovered her fantasies. He obviously didn't mind her secret kinks at all. It wasn't shameful or embarrassing… it was exciting.

What Wendy Wants

Her heart raced, her breathing increased and most of all, despite a delicious spike of fear, adrenaline and anticipation, Wendy felt *happy*.

Being the sole focus of Frank's attention was scary and intoxicating.

Even after that fantastic climax she was still super horny. What a great start to her evening. Frank brought her two-dozen red roses and took her out to a romantic dinner. Then he'd then danced her across the ballroom floor just like Fred Astaire. He'd topped the night off by giving her an amazing orgasm while pressed against a wall.

The man hadn't even taken his clothes off yet. How hot was that?

Wendy had never been so aware of her own *nakedness*.

The slightly abrasive material of his tux felt scratchy, stimulating her bare skin. His palms were big and warm as they brushed against her; his thighs were so thick and strong.

She couldn't help but be hyper-aware of the dominant *maleness* of her sexy husband. He *wanted* her. His stiff erection bulged out in the front of his trousers, she felt it pressing against her.

It was huge. *Yum.*

What Wendy Wants

Her face heated when she recalled how shamelessly she'd humped the palm of his hand. Wendy couldn't recall the last time she'd felt this turned on.

Frank smelled so good and the rough texture of his tux against her bare skin created an erotic tactile craving of its own. Anticipation had her insides churning with a combination of nerves, anxious panic and excitement.

She tried to control her short rapid breaths, but in this bent-over position the blood had rushed to her head.

Her heart hammered in her throat.

For a moment she recalled the 'Giant Canyon' ride she went on once. She'd dangled over a crevice that disappeared thirteen-hundred feet below, swinging at fifty-miles-an-hour over the Colorado River, in Glenwood Springs.

Talk about an adrenaline-pumping rush.

Being on Frank's lap and preparing to receive her first spanking, made her feel just like that.

The words "…her first spanking…" briefly triggered a thrilling thought. If she liked it, surely he'd give her more? Cross fingers, many more.

What Wendy Wants

Right now she felt like she was on the Giant Canyon landing, ready to be thrown off the cliff while listening to other thrill-seekers scream in fright.

Anticipation, anxiety and gut wrenching terror ran like a strange combination of heat and ice in her veins.

Right now, she felt all that and more. Frank was going to spank her. Talk about taking the ride of her life.

"You'd better count each one," he said in his deep, masculine voice. "Ready?"

She cleared her throat. "As I'll ever be."

Slap!

"Owww," Wendy cried out, expelling a sharp breath. The astonishing sound of it echoed loudly in their bedroom.

Reading about a spanking sounded hot, but now that it came down to it, she wasn't so sure. "That really hurt," she gasped.

"It was supposed to. Are you going to count?" he said.

Drawing a deep breath through an open mouth, Wendy filled her lungs and licked her lips. "Um, yes, that was one."

Slap!

What Wendy Wants

"Two!"

Wow. That sharp stinging pain really hurt, but also… it didn't. It left an amazing sensual heat that radiated throughout her whole body.

Wendy found herself panting and squirming. Her entire pelvic area felt heavy and hot with need. The solid feel of Frank's palm slapping against her really did turn her on.

Slap!

"Three!" *God, why do I like this?* she wondered. *But I don't like it. Wait, it hurts! Shit! This is way too hard. Ouch, ow, ouch!*

Slap!

"Four! Red, red, red," she shouted.

Frank stopped instantly. His warm fingers gently stroked her abused buttocks in slow, lazy circles. It was such a soothing caress. He also began blowing on her burning hot ass.

Wendy was panting. The back of her eyes stung with tears.

Emotionally she felt exposed and raw. Physically she was burning hot and tingling all over. Frank kept one strong hand on her shoulder and nape, making her keep still. The other palm gently stroked her sensitive skin.

What Wendy Wants

His touch was like a blaze of heated fire across her flesh. It felt divine. That firm male hand of his was somehow comforting. And super sexy.

In a hitching voice, Wendy panted, "I just needed to catch my breath."

"Tell me how you feel," Frank murmured.

Wendy bit a lip and thought about it. "Everything below my waist is throbbing. It's strange, but do you know, I actually feel better? I don't know why. I guess maybe in my heart of hearts I know I've let you down by enjoying sex without you. I've denied you my body and let us both down. This is kind of making it right. Does that make sense?"

"Totally. Ready for the last painful one?"

"Go ahead."

Slap!

"Owww!" Wendy cried out. That last strike went low on her buttocks. *Shit.* A forceful rush of vibration spiked right through her, pulsing directly into her pelvis and into her womb.

What the hell?

What Wendy Wants

Frank had really let her have it with that last slap and honestly, although it stung like crazy, it still felt good. Maybe because it was the last one?

But no, Frank's pounding punishment felt sensual and amazing. It was maybe like being penetrated hard and fast by a desperate, determined man.

The pain of each strike seamlessly intertwined with erotic pleasure.

She was lost to sensation.

Wendy didn't understand it. It was nuts and it was madness but she wanted him to use that big warm hand of his to spank her again. Each slap caused such an excruciating, edgy, bliss-filled agony.

There was just something incredibly hot about getting a spanking from a big, dominant man.

Her breasts were heavy and swollen. Her pussy ached, it felt *so empty*. Even more than wanting to come, she wanted to spread her legs and to take Frank inside of her. She wanted to accept and surrender *to him*.

To anything he wanted.

To everything he wanted.

What Wendy Wants

With each strike, despite the pain, her thighs tightened and her inner muscles convulsed with wicked, forbidden ecstasy. She was so turned on that her entire body shook. She'd finally experienced a spanking and it felt remarkable.

"What did you forget?" Frank intoned in a mockingly severe voice.

"Um, I don't know." Wendy whimpered. Sincerely.

"If *you* don't count, *they* don't count," he said, his voice deep with authority and control.

Wendy took a moment while she tried to comprehend what Frank was talking about. Her entire body throbbed. It was difficult to think when her backside was on fire, and her pussy pulsed with need.

When she suddenly realized what Frank meant, she felt a bubble of hysterical laughter push up through her chest.

Just how many of her erotic books had he read, anyway? Tonight was like every fantasy she'd ever imagined all rolled into one. Her husband was a quick learner, but this was really impressive, even for him.

She briefly considered refusing, just to see what he'd do. Or maybe pleading ignorance to extend the sweet torture, but finally she decided that she'd better be good. This time.

What Wendy Wants

"Oh. Um, five?"

"Good girl. Now you're supposed to thank me for your punishment," he said, following what he'd read as exactly as possible.

"Thank you, for spanking me," she said meekly, but she the words she said were heartfelt.

"You did just great, sweetheart," Frank praised, his voice husky with desire, his hands and fingers trailing a sweet, sexy fire along her heated flesh.

His breathing was ragged with effort and lust. Raw passion emanated from him, a sensual energy that seemed to seep into her.

Her husband *wanted* her. Wendy found his primal male need for her captivating.

When you're with someone who cares about you; someone that *you* care about, every pleasure is heightened. The sexual act becomes an expression of love. For that reason everything is much more intense.

Wendy was already in love with Frank.

Just then, she fell in love with her husband all over again.

Tears stung her eyes for another reason now, but damned if she could explain why. Frank fulfilled her crazy longing to experience a spanking. He was extremely turned on, but there was something in his voice.

Pride? Happiness? Love?

But his hands were upon her again, caressing her, soothing her, stroking her buttocks and now between her legs. Jesus, it felt so good. Her clit throbbed, her whole body was sensitive and alive.

"Damn, woman, you're flooding down here. My trousers are soaked. I think you liked being spanked."

Wendy exhaled a long, slow breath. "I'm still trying to figure it out, but I think I did, too. There's just something wicked and sexy… and would you believe, *loving* about it?"

"Loving?"

"I feel loved," she sniffed. "I can't believe that you did this for me, Frank."

"I'd do anything for you, Wendy," he said gruffly.

Man, she had to change the subject of she'd start crying again. She cleared her throat. "I feel as if I'm burning hot all over."

"You're hot, alright," he snickered.

What Wendy Wants

Still lying across his lap, she grinned up at him and added, "I also really want you to fuck me."

"That's good," he said with a dark chuckle. "Really good, but I'm not going to fuck you yet."

Vibrator

Wendy

~~~

She bit her lip so she wouldn't whine like a little girl, even though she wanted to.

Hyper-aware of Frank, Wendy felt him reach down for something beside him. Her breath caught when she felt him slide a soft object into her drenched pussy. It was horseshoe shaped and one part of it rested upon her clit.

"This is a We-Vibe 3 vibrator," Frank said.

She snickered. "You brought me a vibrator?" she asked. "What a thoughtful gift." She realized that he must have had a remote for it because it suddenly turned on in a low, pleasurable pulsation. Her instant harsh gasp sounded loud to her ears.

"Do you like it?" he crooned.

"For the love of God, Frank," she panted. "I love it. God, honey, I'm so close to climax again already."

"That's great. I told you I planned to make you scream didn't I?"

What Wendy Wants

Wendy found herself hardly able to answer, she could only pant and moan breathlessly.

"So, good, honey. This feels so good."

He chuckled. "This vibrator is supposed to hit the woman's G spot while stimulating their clit at the same time," he told her conversationally.

Wendy heard him, but found it difficult to concentrate. Every brain cell she had was focused where that lovely pulsing sensation was.

Frank's head bend down, where he seemed to be checking the position of her toy. Apparently satisfied, he straightened.

"Keep your legs together to hold on to the vibrator. It's going to feel amazing inside while I spank you. You don't have to count now, this spanking is for pleasure. I want to see if I can make you come with a spanking while using this toy."

Wendy had to giggle. "Seriously? My backside is already throbbing and stinging, but I'm game."

Frank ran his fingers beneath her hair, caressing her nape. "Well, *I'm* having fun, sweetheart. Making you come is the hottest thing in the world for me. And this is just the start of our adventures."

"Oh, Frank, I'm so glad."

What Wendy Wants

Slap! Slap! Slap!

Rhythmically Frank's hand softly struck her, sending shockwaves through her body. Each strike of his hand made her pussy clench in a pulsing wave of desire. This spanking was sensual and erotic, but that could be because of the sexy vibrating pressure in her pussy and on her clit.

He stopped spanking for a bit, instead caressing and stroking. "Look at me, Wendy," he said and she turned her head, craning to see him. "Do you like it?" he asked, his shrewd, knowing eyes filled with lust.

"It feels incredible," she whispered.

"I like it, too," he murmured. Frank upped the vibrator speed and Wendy sucked in a lungful of air so fast that she almost choked.

"How's that?" he asked.

"Oh, God," she said breathlessly.

"Good," Frank said. "I'm going to keep spanking and changing the vibrator setting around. Tell me what you like, but you don't get to come until I say."

His voice lowered. "I want to hear you beg for it, just like in all those damn books of yours."

What Wendy Wants

"Shall I start begging now?" she asked. "I want to."

He laughed. "No. Hold on until you're desperate."

"I'm already desperate," she whined.

"Too bad. You have to wait for it, sweetheart."

He kept up a steady, predictable rhythm, slow at first, and then faster, alternating cheeks. Like the strokes one might receive from a desperately horny man during intercourse, slap, slap, slap, slap.

Wendy began to pant. Skin against skin, every strike felt good in a wickedly wanton, yet vulnerable way. She was writhing with pleasure, writhing with pain. The burn and heat of it was building into something amazing. That vibrator kept her on the cusp of climax, she was so close!

Wendy cried out after one sharp slap.

Frank stopped. "Okay?" he asked.

"God, yes!"

He chuckled. "Good."

"Please, please may I come?"

"Nope. Hold still. I'm not done yet."

Slap! Slap! Slap!

What Wendy Wants

The burning heat of it went straight to her pussy — so did the sensual vibrations.

Wendy found that she wanted *more*. More agonizing pleasure.

More of that hard stinging hand.

More of *him*.

Her husband was big and strong and he was holding her down… making her submit.

Dominating her.

It felt *so fucking hot*. Wendy panted. She squirmed and whimpered and moaned. The vibrator felt fantastic.

The scent of her own arousal filled the air, that and the masculine smell of Frank and his sexy cologne.

Her body quivered, her belly clenched and her womb wept while Frank delivered slaps to her ass, one cheek, then the other. The low level sting was both exquisite and excruciating. It made everything from her waist down throb with heat and ache for release.

Sharp waves of intense sensation rolled through her, making her shudder.

What Wendy Wants

"Frank, please I need to come," she gasped. "I don't think I can stop it!"

"Soon," he said.

Wendy felt his hard hand and the press of his hard dick. There was no doubt about it, Frank was enjoying spanking her.

She imagined herself as he would see her, her white ass red with multiple handprints, trembling and shaking, while she fidgeted and wriggled against his strong thighs and cock, enduring his blows.

Accepting *everything*.

"Frank," she cried out desperately, surprised that she'd been capable of even saying his name.

"Come for me, sweetheart," he growled. "Let me see it, let me hear how much you like what I'd doing. I want to see you come."

Everything coiled and tightened.

Oh, God! Her whole body began to shudder.

At that exact moment Frank turned the vibrator that was stimulating her G spot and clit to high pulse. He gave her two more hard strikes.

Slap! Slap!

What Wendy Wants

Her pussy was molten. Her ass was on fire.

White-hot heat rolled through her. For an instant her mind went blank. She let go completely as pleasure and pain combined into something indescribable.

Wendy screamed and her whole body stiffened as she was engulfed by a blast of sensual bliss. Her pussy spasmed, pulsing and pulsing. Her scream turned into a wail as she came apart.

The vibrator kept going.

It was too much! Excruciating. It hurt *so good*. When that peak ended, before she was able to catch her breath, she seemed to start on another.

Wendy was caught in a powerful maelstrom of sensation. Each convulsion was like a tiny seizure of its own: contraction, contraction, contraction – they went on and on.

Was this a multiple orgasm?

If so it was her first.

Wendy climaxed so hard and for so long that her vision darkened. For a moment she feared that she may lose consciousness.

Never before had she experienced such rapture.

What Wendy Wants

It was ecstasy.

Ecstasy!

Mindless with bliss, she was barely aware when Frank stopped spanking her and turned the vibrator off. He held her down while she bucked and writhed, preventing her from falling to the floor.

She lost a bit of time there somehow, because suddenly she seemed to be sitting on his lap, cradled protectively within Frank's arms.

He gently tended her, stroking, kissing and petting while she came back to herself.

Wendy felt disembodied… it was as if she was floating.

Wow, that was *intense!* She'd heard stories that women experienced the greatest sexual pleasure when they hit forty. She was two years off that now.

Holy shit.

I just had the most powerful orgasm of my whole life. If there's something more intense coming in a couple of years, I'm not sure that I'll survive it!

~What Wendy Wants~

Frank's Fantasy

Frank

~~~

His heart kicked with a flood of adrenaline as he pulled his wife back up to return to sitting on his lap. He held her with both arms, afraid that she may fall off.

He'd been seriously concerned that he'd really hurt her. That scream of Wendy's had been so loud and anguished that for a second there he wouldn't have been surprised to find that he'd accidentally given her a heart attack or stroke.

"Are you okay?" he asked, when she'd recovered somewhat. It was difficult to hide the anxiety in his voice.

Wendy just stared vaguely at him with dilated pupils. Her eyes were glazed and heavy-lidded. She looked languid and dreamy, as if she was tripped out from drugs.

"Honey," she murmured and said nothing more.

"Yes?" he encouraged, waiting another beat.

"That was the most intense climax that I've ever had."

What Wendy Wants

Frank smiled so hard that he felt the strain of it on his face. "Really?"

"Oh, yeah," she said in a tone of awe. "I swear it. I think I've had multiple orgasms now, something I've read about but never experienced."

"How many?" he asked curiously.

She grinned. "Two. Three, maybe. I don't know. I thought I was going to pass out there for a minute because I couldn't catch my breath between them."

They discussed her spanking for a bit, with Frank plying her with questions about what turned her on and what didn't.

Wendy began to detail how overwhelming it had been and how he'd done everything perfectly, not too hard, not too soft.

Frank found her forthright appraisal really satisfying. Later he would tell his new friends on FetLife exactly how it went and thank them for being so helpful.

The spanking had absolutely made her hot.

Surprisingly, it made him horny as hell, too.

What Wendy Wants

What was that about? Seeing her writhe as she accepted his punishment? Making her buttocks red? The fact that she was completely in his power? Who knew?

The vibrator was a real hit. Frank intended to make Wendy climax some more, but just now his balls were aching. He needed relief and he wanted to come in her mouth. How would a Dom in one of those books react?

Suddenly he knew.

"I want you to kneel for me now," he growled with intentionally bold confidence.

Wendy reacted with a grin, instantly dropping to her knees between his legs. Frank slid to the edge of the chair and took off his tux jacket.

He didn't plan on getting naked just yet, but he was too warm. He rolled up his sleeves to cool himself off and to let her know that he still meant business.

It was a subtle message. He was still in control and he planned to get busy again real soon.

To get to work *on her*.

She looked at him intently while licking her lips.

What Wendy Wants

The thought of those soft lips of hers made more blood shoot into his already painfully hard dick. The knowledge that he was possibly going to ejaculate in her mouth for the first time made everything down low, from his gut and below, tighten.

"Take my cock out," he instructed, still seated on the chair.

"Oh, Frank, you commanding tough guy, you," Wendy cooed when she reached for his zip and freed his aching erection. "God almighty, honey, you have no idea what words like that do for me. You make me so freaking horny."

Wendy held his cock, reverently stroking it.

Frank watched her. Wendy's eyes never left him. This gave him a huge thrill, because she was waiting for instructions. She was looking at him, wanting to be directed on exactly how to best please him.

Frank gripped her nape and pulled her to his cock.

"Lick it and suck it," he said and she nodded her agreement. Wendy took him inside of her and he shut his eyes, simply enjoying the sensation of her working him with her wet, hot mouth.

"Yes, that's perfect," he said in a deep whisper. "God, it's so good, baby."

What Wendy Wants

Wendy's breath was warm upon his balls as she sucked and released, sucked and released, her tongue running around his ridges. Frank figured that he could take this all night.

Wendy looked happy, too. She began to hum with pleasure, using her hand, her lips and her tongue.

That humming of hers added sensual vibration to his blow job. His entire shaft was pulsing as she bobbed her head up and down on him.

Hot damn, it feels incredible.

Frank withstood her efforts as long as he could, but he felt drunk with lust and ready to come.

Heart pounding, breath ragged, he stood up, needing more control. With both hands he grabbed her hair, twisting it into a firm grip.

Hair pulling 57% he thought absently.

Most of his focus was on her mouth and his throbbing cock.

Wendy moaned and began vacuuming him in, working him harder and deeper.

Can she climax while sucking me off? he wondered. *Because she sure looks to be on the edge again already.*

What Wendy Wants

Using her hair as leverage, Frank held her head still and began fucking her mouth. The feel of his hands in her hair, pulling against her scalp created erotic, tactile delight. Sliding between her full red lips, in and out, in and out, he went as deep as she seemed capable of taking him.

It felt divine.

Seeing her on her knees before him, the sight of her naked except for those stockings, black garters and red heels, the euphoric look on her face as she gladly accepted his cock, the smell and feel of her…it was all too much.

He was going to realize his fantasy.

Frank was thrilled by the idea of spurting right down her throat.

"I'm going to come," he rasped, as he felt his building climax reach its peak. "I want you to take it – take it all. And swallow every fucking drop."

With her lips around his dick, Wendy couldn't speak. She gazed up at him and her eyes flared with desire.

Frank's deep inhalation of pleasure and surprise sounded loud in the small room.

He easily read her body language.

What Wendy Wants

Wendy wanted it.

She wanted to take his cum and drink him down.

That thought broke the last of his control. Frank felt his muscles bunch and flex, thighs, stomach and ass clenching as the force and his violence of his release took him.

Hips jerking ruthlessly, Frank drove hard into Wendy's wet and willing mouth.

"Uh, oh," he grunted in pulse-pounding pleasure. Wendy moaned as he convulsively shot his load, once, twice, three times, emptying himself inside of her. His thighs tightened and legs shook.

It was sensual bliss. It was heaven.

Frank saw her eyes widen with what? Surprise? No. Her face lit, she seemed transported with delight. She wanted his cum. She'd enjoyed swallowing it, taking every drop.

Something about that one act gave him an extraordinary sense of joy and fulfillment. Why was that?

Some might imagine that having his wife on her knees giving him a blow job and swallowing was wrong or dirty or subservient.

It was none of those things.

What Wendy Wants

Wrong, dirty and subservient. He smiled for a moment and considered that it was actually *all of those things.*

Perhaps that was what made it so damn hot. But mainly her submission to his carnal desires was beyond price.

It was a gift.

Frank wondered if there were enough words in the English language to possibly describe how he was feeling right now. He'd brought his wife to mind-numbing ecstasy and she'd done the same for him.

The sense of love and connection he felt toward her was intense.

How could he explain to her how he felt?

Only a catalog of terms *might* come close. Words such as godlike, masculine, satisfied, virile, invigorated, contented, needed, valued, primal, primitive and caveman all would be on the list.

Frank fell back down onto the chair, his hand still possessively gripping his wife's nape and pulling her close, capturing her between his thighs.

So many potent feelings and a million possible ways to describe them.

What Wendy Wants

His chest was tight with wonder and awe. Was it possible to articulate this swelling sense of euphoria to his wife?

Neither Wendy nor Frank spoke for long moments.

The bedroom still flickered with light, perfumed with the vanilla scent of candles and the heady musk of sex. The sound of ragged breathing from both of them was all that could be heard.

How can I explain these powerful emotions?

"Fuck, that was incredible," Frank finally said.

Those few words didn't even come close, yet it was all he could think of to say.

It would have to do.

Connection

Frank

~~~

Reaching down, he embraced Wendy, pulling her to her feet and kissing her. Wrapping his arms around her, he felt her whole body melt against him. What words couldn't express, maybe the intimacy of a kiss could.

He wasn't sure how long they remained wrapped around each other, but while their kiss was passionate, it wasn't only sexual.

"I really love you, you know that?" Frank said when he pulled away from her.

Tears were running down her face. Wendy was crying, emotional girl that she was. She was also smiling, so that was okay.

Frank curled her into him again, caressing and calming his beautiful wife. She wasn't a small woman; it was just that he was so much bigger.

"I'm so lucky to have you, sweetheart," he said.

Those tears flowed faster and her weeping got louder. He tipped her chin up.

What Wendy Wants

"Now what is going on? You're happy, right?"

Wendy's breath hitched and she said, "I'm really happy."

Frank laughed, swept her up into his arms and stood up.

He was feeling pretty damn emotional himself, but he was nowhere near crying. He figured that as a woman, Wendy must have a hundred percent of some 'feeling' or 'emotional' gene that he only had five percent of.

Taking her over to the bed, he lay her down gently.

Frank handing her a box of tissues. Tracks of tears ran down her cheeks.

Smiling down at her, he began to undress, taking everything off and sliding on to the bed with her, pulling her on top of his chest. He patted and soothed and let her finish her emotional jag.

There was no rush. He'd be happy to enjoy this open closeness with his wife forever.

"Better?" He said when she seemed to have exhausted her astonishing supply of tears.

Wendy nodded.

What Wendy Wants

"Are you able to explain why you're crying?" he said, his lips curling in a wry smile.

Wendy sniffed and blew her nose. Frank felt his smile grow larger. Damn, she was just too adorable.

"It's just…I just have really missed this, Frank," she said. "This intimacy. I don't really understand how it slipped away from us. I couldn't be happier right now. I feel so connected."

They had a longer conversation then.

Frank admitted how he'd gravitated toward internet XXX rated sites almost daily and pay channel porn when he was away on business trips. He also told her about masturbating daily in the shower.

"Throughout our marriage I've wanted you to suck me off and swallow my cum," he admitted."

"Why didn't you tell me?"

"Probably for similar reasons that you found it hard to talk to me about your fantasies. I thought it was too dirty, wrong maybe and perverse. I didn't want you to think less of me."

Wendy frowned. "I would never think less of you, hon."

Still uncomfortable, he looked away from her penetrating gaze while he reflected and tried to pull his thoughts together.

"I'd considered that maybe only," he cleared his throat, "a certain type of women let a man come in their mouth. To ask for… that, well, it seemed like disrespecting you."

"Wow," she said, "but I loved it."

"You can't know how happy that makes me."

He grinned at her and she grinned back.

"I've never, well, no one has ever done that with me." He gave a depreciating snort. "I wasn't exactly a stud before I met you."

She looked down at his cock, already fully erect and laughed. "You've always been a stud, hon. You've just never been an over-experienced, jaded sexual player."

"I'm making up for it now. Was it… was it really okay for you?"

"I loved it," she said, her eyes glowing. "I felt powerful, kind of like only I had the ability to give you what you need maybe. I don't know. It was amazing to hear and see and *feel* you come. To realize, 'I did that.' But also, I think I loved it because *you* loved it."

He kissed her nose. "I didn't think I'd enjoy spanking you, but it was seriously hot to feel you struggle while I held you down and delivered that punishment. The physicality of it, the look of your red ass, and the feel of heat on my palm? It was out of this world. What I was doing made you so damn wet that you drenched my trousers. The whole damn thing was erotic as hell. But I mostly think I loved it because *you* did."

My beautiful wife's face flushed, not with embarrassment, but with fresh sensual heat. Oh yeah. I'd be spanking her again real soon.

A philosophical discussion ensued about right and wrong, and good and bad. Also things to be ashamed of, and things to be feel guilty about. Could anything carried out between two consensual adults be wrong? And why should they be embarrassed by something a loving partner wanted to try?

Right then they made a pact to never lie to each other, and to live out their sexual fantasies together.

Was it easier to be truthful about such things to strangers? He didn't think so. If two intelligent, loving, and happily married people couldn't be honest with each other about their most hidden sexual desires, then who could?

Frank didn't know if he was technically a Dom, but he definitely enjoyed dominating her. Wendy didn't know if she was genuinely submissive, but she certainly loved submitting to him.

"Arms over your head and part your thighs," Frank ordered, remembering the exact command from one of her stories. He wanted to go down on her now, and make her climax again.

What Wendy Wants

Wendy did as she was ordered. Frank kissed and licked his way down her body. He spread her legs further and gave her clit the first lash of his tongue.

"Frank," she cried out, tensing and pulling her legs together.

"What?" he asked, while removing her stockings, her garters and high heels.

Wendy didn't answer immediately and Frank said, "No secrets, baby, what's the matter?"

"Maybe I should have a shower first," she said tentatively.

Frank laughed. Wasn't that just like a woman? To worry about something like that? Next she would be telling him to blow out the candles because she was too fat to be seen naked.

"Sweetheart," he said. "You had a shower already today. To me, you smell great. You taste great, too."

"Seriously?"

"No joke," he said and he wasn't lying. To him she was sweet and slick and fantastic. "But there's one problem. These candles aren't bright enough."

Frank got up, turned on all the lights in the bedroom, and returned to kneel between her legs. "I want to see what I'm doing."

What Wendy Wants

"Frank, no," Wendy shrieked her disapproval, protesting fiercely, struggling as he slid his hands up the inside of her legs and spread her thighs.

Frank ignored her.

With his strength he easily subdued her, pressing her against the mattress. His no-nonsense gaze pinned her down.

"Are you going to stop me?" He asked with a deceptively mild voice.

She met his eyes for a moment and looked away. "No," she said.

"Don't be ashamed, sweetheart. Why should you be? Your husband wants to have a good, close look between his wife's legs."

"It's embarrassing," she said.

"You'll get past that. I think you're beautiful down here."

Still tense, Wendy covered her face.

It seemed that she objected to such close scrutiny. Too bad. Curious man that he was, Frank wanted to see her most feminine parts in order to get them straight in his mind. He also wanted to watch and learn what happened during arousal and orgasm.

What Wendy Wants

She was clearly uncomfortable and struggling with having her legs spread wide with the lights on. Taking her clit between his teeth, he gently bit down.

Wendy stilled the moment his mouth was upon her.

With his face against her flesh, he smiled wickedly. He'd hold still too if their positions were reversed and she had his cock between her teeth.

He pressed against her, opened his mouth wide and began to suck and flick her captured clit with his tongue. She whimpered.

Who could resist the sensation of a warm tongue flicking against their most sensitive, private parts?

"Oh," she gasped loudly. The tension in her body relaxed as the fight went out of her.

Now a different kind of tension was beginning to coil inside.

Frank knew that every nerve and muscle in his wife's genitals, pelvis, buttocks and thighs would increase with excruciating tension. It would continue to build right until her body released it all at once in another series of pleasurable waves. Not counting multiples, this would be her third orgasm for the night.

He took his time, parting her with his fingers, enjoying the lush swell of her mound and vulva, while running his tongue along her entry.

What Wendy Wants

To his delight she squirmed and panted and groaned.

He spread her nether lips open with his thumbs and laved her, stopping from time to time to look, study and analyze her girlie bits. *Mons pubis, labia majora, labia minora, clitoral hood,* he recited, checking every intimate detail.

Right now her vaginal area and clitoris were incredibly swollen, thick with blood. Like men, apparently women suffered pelvic heaviness and aching if they experienced foreplay but didn't reach climax.

There were different types of orgasms, clitoral, vaginal and many combinations of the two.

According to surveys he'd read, only twenty-five percent of women *always* climax during sex with a partner. Hit – or miss – was normal for the other seventy-five percent, and some of those woman apparently *never* experienced an orgasm during intercourse.

That fact still shocked him.

When he slid a finger into her while sucking her clit, she became louder. The wonderful sounds of her soft sighs, whimpers and moans made him hard and ready.

He kept this sensual torment up until her head flailed back and forth, her body thrashed and she fisted the sheets.

What Wendy Wants

"Fuck me, Frank. I want you inside of me," she begged constantly, a desperate chorus of pleas.

"No," he growled. "I'm the one in charge here, remember? I'll fuck you when I'm good and ready to fuck you."

"Then will you at least let me come?" she pleaded.

"Not yet."

"You're such a bully," she snapped at him.

He just laughed. This was her fantasy. The kind of stuff that *she* had highlighted on her Kindle. She wanted a dominant alpha male that made the heroine wait for it, driving them to desperation and making them beg.

He'd spent the time and done his study. Frank had always been a good student. Other than if she used her safeword, the Dom, had all the control during sex. Wendy had to learn patience.

This new game he was playing was *fun*. Toying with her entry and licking her clit, he felt as if he could do this for hours.

Every time Frank saw and felt her close to the edge he held back, stopping her from going over.

What Wendy Wants

He examined her clitoris. She was so hyper-excited that her clitoris had already retracted under the 'clitoral hood' and had become inaccessible to direct stimulation.

Blood continued to flood into her pelvic area, her breath sped up, her heart rate increased to a rapid pant, while her nipples had stiffened, begging for his attention. Frank couldn't see it, but he knew that the lower part of her vagina would have narrowed, preparing to grip his dick during climax.

No dick for her right now.

He planned to make her come with his tongue.

Wendy arched, attempting to push closer, bowing toward him, but his strong firm hands held her exactly where he wanted.

He finally allowed her to climax once more, this time with his tongue curled deep inside of her.

Frank felt every second of her climax while counting her contractions.

Licking the taste of her from his lips, he gave her a short break to recover before he climbed on top of her. She was still shuddering with aftershocks, but now it was his turn.

What Wendy Wants

With a bit of luck, maybe he could make her come again. This time he would feed that hungry cunt of hers his cock. He looked forward to feeling her grip him as she came.

Neanderthal

Frank

~~~

They both moaned when he fell upon her, his lips passionately meeting hers. The smell and feel of her skin, her mouth, in fact her whole body made him feel savage in his need.

Frank felt as if he could devour her.

"Put your arms around me, baby, and hold on tight," he breathed against her ear. She did, one arm curled around his neck and one circling his back. He notched himself against her wet and welcoming entry. Then he thrust deep inside, his balls tight against her.

He grunted with the exquisite pleasure of it. Wendy called out something unintelligible and her internal muscles squeezed him, clamping down *hard*.

Pausing, Frank held perfectly still, while trying to slow his breathing.

"Sweetheart," he said roughly, his body trembling as he rested on his arms. "I can't be gentle."

"I want it hard" – pant – "and fast" – pant – "and I want it now!"

What Wendy Wants

"Oh, shit," he gasped. He was a big, strong and violently aroused man, but Wendy had given the okay. There was no reason to restrain himself. Just like an animal that had slipped its chain, he didn't hold back.

He pulled out and then slammed back inside, again and again, making her whole body jerk with each brutal thrust. With unrestrained passion, Frank rode her hard, driving in deep while seeking release.

Even then he'd already trained himself to be hyperaware of her response to him and her reactions. He listened to her breathing, the feel of her body and the noises of arousal that she made.

Like anyone else, he screwed up from time to time, but he learned from his mistakes. From now on, whenever he made love he would always be aware of his wife.

The rhythmic suck and pull as he fucked her made slapping liquid sounds, adding to his animal pleasure.

Wendy was making noise again, sighs, whimpers and moans. Her nails dug into his flesh, scratching his back.

It felt amazing.

Frank's cock throbbed and twitched against the walls of her tight, swollen channel.

What Wendy Wants

"Jesus, I'm going to give it to you," he growled as he neared his crest.

As he felt himself going over the edge he grabbed her backside. Frank's fingers bit into her as he lifted her up further to meet his thrusts. He drove inside as deep as he could go, again and again with bruising force.

Wendy cried out, a wanton needy sound that went right through him, directly to his cock and balls. In this position, he knew his pubic bone was rubbing her clit. Chest heaving, Frank's entire body corded with strain.

He grunted as shudders wracked his frame when he ejaculated.

As he emptied himself inside of her, shooting his hot seed, over and over, Frank felt Wendy climax with him, tightening and loosening.

During the last of his release, her body convulsed, her internal muscles clamping down hard around his erection, causing incredible ripples of sensation. With his balls already empty, he came once more in a completely dry climax.

It felt amazing. Excruciatingly amazing, but still fucking good.

Could anything be better?

What Wendy Wants

Totally spent, Frank lay on her, waiting to catch his breath. His cock stayed deep inside, occasionally throbbing and twitching. Sated, he rested there absorbing the exquisite sensation of Wendy's tight channel pulsing with aftershocks.

Arms still wrapped around each other, they remained bound to each other, both panting and sweating. It had been as if they were one person as they reached that pinnacle of pleasure together.

His wife looked tousled, well-used and utterly satisfied. Nuzzling into her, he breathed her in. After a long, languorous moment, Frank rolled off her and went to the bathroom for a washcloth and towel.

At first Wendy murmured her protest, but Frank overruled it and continued what he was doing. He took his time, cleaning and drying between her legs.

This is what guys in those books often did and he could see why.

There was nothing embarrassing about it for him or her, or at least there shouldn't be. It was an intimate and loving action. In cleaning and drying Wendy, felt as if he was *caring* for his wife.

This perfect woman is mine, he thought, awed by the truth of it.

Knowing this made something in his chest tighten. 'She is mine' came up in those erotic books over and over. Wendy wanted him to have this proprietary feeling for her, this need to claim her as his.

What Wendy Wants

He wanted it, too.

Frank smiled. It was so damn Neanderthal.

He climbed back into bed, wrapped his arms around her and pulled her onto his chest.

Boneless, Wendy gave a soft sigh of contented pleasure. Their bodies slid together naturally, seamlessly. She belonged in his arms.

This whole night had been perfect.

When Wendy finally came back to herself, they held each other in a loving embrace. Curious, he got up and brought her Kindle back to bed. They both knew what had inspired Frank's sudden desire to dominate her.

"I want to ask you about this," he said and showed her what she'd highlighted in *'Karma.'*

"Oh," she said. "Well, I took what he said to heart. There were a few things that really registered with me. Things like: **"Knowing that your lover understands you, and you understand him is important."**

Frank smiled. "We have lots more to learn and appreciate about each other, but we're moving in the right direction now. What else?"

What Wendy Wants

"Oh, some of these words like *'honest skin-to-skin, soul-to-soul connection.'* I also realized that the fact that you get hard for me and desire me is a real turn on. When I read this was the first time that I considered how hot it would be to be on my knees. To have you order me to take it in my mouth."

"Really? Man, this is almost too good to be true."

Wendy laughed, grinning broadly. No doubt realized how hot she made him while on her knees and taking his cum.

"Anyway," she said. "I just highlighted it because I figured that if I ever got up my nerve I'd tell you what I wanted to try. I'm such a coward. I just never got the courage to tell you."

Frank pulled her to him again. This time he swung her on top of him, holding her by the waist while she straddled him.

"You look fantastic, wife," he said.

"You look pretty damn edible yourself, husband," she said.

By the end of the night they had cuddled, talked and made love for hours.

It had been better than during their honeymoon.

The last time Frank made love to her, not with dominance and submission, but romantically, lovingly, soft and slow.

What Wendy Wants

His mouth came down on hers, swallowing her cries of pleasure. Her body was soft, her skin hot and ready. Strong and deep, he pushed into her, while she wrapped herself around him.

They whispered endearments to each other as they caressed each other's bodies.

She was so damn sexy.

Frank worshiped her, telling her with his lips and hands just how important she was to him. He felt the tight walls of her channel with every thrust. Wendy trembled and she quivered just before her release.

Her orgasm triggered his own so that in the end they climaxed together

Even though he hadn't been very romantic in a long time, Frank loved romance. He loved seduction and kissing and cuddling. But this dominance and submission stuff was a hell of a lot of fun, too.

In the final analysis they lost track of the number of orgasms Wendy experienced. Frank informed her that he'd reliably counted five, with a multiple orgasm possibility of seven.

Stubborn and determined, Frank had achieved his objective.

He'd found what Wendy wanted and had given her *exactly that*.

What Wendy Wants

He hadn't even had the opportunity to use any novelty items while making love – except for that vibrator. There were still so many sex toys available in his little bag of tricks that he'd bought from 'The Crypt.'

Frank smiled as he and his wife wrapped themselves around each other, tangled together while drifting off to sleep.

Unconsciously, already asleep, Wendy snuggled into his arms

Cuffs? Bondage? Blindfolds? Well, there's always next time, he thought with a deeply satisfied sigh. *Maybe we can try that in the morning before we pick up the boys.*

After that thought he fell almost instantly asleep.

Aftermath

Frank

~~~

They both slept in.

Frank woke in the morning light, achingly aroused. Physically he felt better than ever. Oh, he was a little sore from using muscles in interesting ways that he didn't usually use them, but he was also incredibly happy.

With a slow smile, he immediately reached for his wife.

This was a completely new behavior. In the past he hid his erections and attended to them himself without disturbing Wendy.

All that was going to change now.

Wendy lay on her side, turned away from him. It was easy to snuggle up, spooning against her.

He'd read somewhere that a good dominant uses seduction to gain consent. With that in mind, Frank decided that he simply had to get his wife interested and she'd be up for anything.

He stroked her awake, erotically caressing the sensitive skin of her nape.

What Wendy Wants

"Mm," she murmured. "Good morning."

"Shush," he said, with sudden inspiration. "You're asleep."

She tilted her head back to look at him. "I am?" she asked in a playful tone.

"Yes, you most certainly are. This is a dream, sweetheart. A very sexy dream."

"Ah, I see." She smiled. "Okay."

Wasn't there a story where a man pretended that his lover was asleep? It sounded pretty erotic, so that's what Frank decided he'd do, too.

With gentle fingers, in a slow, soft approach, he rubbed and stroked her back, arms and shoulders. Tactile pleasures for her to enjoy; his chest against her back, the hard length of his erection pressing against her buttocks

She made a cute mewling sound.

Hyper-alert to her every response, Frank noticed *everything*. Her heart rate had increased, her skin was flushed, and her breathing had changed. When he ran his hands over her breasts her nipples puckered as he flicked and teased them.

Wendy whimpered and sighed with her growing arousal. His already swollen cock got harder.

"You're asleep, remember," he whispered into her ear while his probing fingers continued to tease and caress her. "You're having an erotic dream. But I've found this beautiful, sleeping woman and I'm going to play with her exactly as I want to."

To his delight, Wendy gave him a breathy moan.

Frank ran his hand through her hair, winding his fingers into her locks and pulling on them, creating an erotic nip of sensation. All the while he continued kissing and nibbling his way along her throat and jaw and back again.

Hair pulling 57% Neck/ nape bite/ nuzzle 55%.

She tasted salty and sweet. He licked behind her ear and blew softly on her moistened skin. He took her earlobe between his teeth and bit it.

Wendy exhaled in a hiss, then whimpered. It was a desperate sound. When she shifted her legs apart to give him more access, he smiled.

"Don't wake up yet, gorgeous," he whispered. "I want to finger your tight little cunt."

As he'd come to expect, he was rewarded with a sharp intake of breath. A gasp, really, and he loved it.

He traced her flank, caressing the yielding round globes of her bottom, then down the back of her thighs.

What Wendy Wants

Her skin was warm, smooth silk. His hand burrowed between her legs from behind her, pushing past her buttocks and reaching into her wet cleft, fingering and teasing.

Whenever she responded he repeated whatever caused the reaction, lazily lingering there until she reacted again and again with quiet whimpers or moans.

Wendy's chest was rising and falling, short and fast. She was virtually panting and he'd barely even touched her. She was also making lots of incoherent, sexy sounds.

He brought her damp fingers to his nose and breathed in. "I love your seductive, musky scent." He placed his fingers in his mouth. "I love your taste, too," he said, his voice guttural with lust.

"God, Frank," she gasped. "Alright already! It's time for me to wake up."

He laughed. "No one makes me feel the way you do, sweetheart. I need to be inside of you *right now*."

"You won't hear any complaints from me," she giggled.

She quivered when he lifted her leg to give himself access, and then he drove himself inside of her.

What Wendy Wants

They started slow, sweet and easy, graced with soft whispers of love and tenderness. As they surged together, the sound of their ragged breaths sounded loud in the empty room.

Frank was surprised at how quickly their tensions mounted to breaking point.

"I'm going to come," she gasped as his thighs slammed against her ass.

"Good. Come. Come now," he growled.

When Frank's fingers toyed along her soft folds and flicked her clit, she climaxed, crying out and clamping down on him again and again.

Once again, her release prompted his own. He grunted as he thrust, driving deeply into her as he came.

They lay together in the afterglow of orgasm, enjoying each other's company.

"Mmmm," she said. "That's a nice way to wake up."

"I agree." His dick, still deep inside of her, twitched. From time to time her pussy did too. She sighed and it was a sweet sound, a confirmation that all was right in their world.

What Wendy Wants

"I've been a good father, but a bad husband," he mused out loud. "I took you for granted, sweetheart. I swear that will never happen again."

Wendy rolled over toward him. "I'm the one that's been avoiding you in bed."

He stroked her hair in an intentionally soothing caress, acknowledging her.

Wendy threw her arms around his neck in a warm embrace, running her fingers through his hair, curling into it and tugging. He ran his nose up along her throat to her cheek, pressing soft feather-like kisses against her.

"I'm sorry, hon," she whispered, her breath soft against him.

"Don't be."

This caring and loving attention, each to the other, was something like an apology. Frank understood and he wanted her to know it. After he kissed her forehead he held his face against hers.

With his nose in her hair he just breathed her in.

"It's okay, sweetheart," he said with a sigh, finally lying back and pulling her into his arms. "I blame myself. I haven't been satisfying you,

What Wendy Wants

I get that now. But from now on, whatever you want, whatever you need, I want to be there to give it to you."

"It's my fault, too, Frank."

He grinned at her. "It sure is. Isn't it amazing how stupid this is? How we fell into an almost comfy kind of marital melancholy?"

The phone rang.

"Crap," Frank said. The digital clock beside the bed said it was almost nine am. "I'll get it."

"Hello?"

"Hi Frank. It's Dawn. Did you two have a good time last night?"

He looked at his wife, all hair-tousled and flushed in their bed. "We had a wonderful time. I can't thank you enough."

Wendy got up and took the phone from him.

Saturday morning, day off. What a perfect start to the day. He put on some jeans, left his wife talking to her sister and went down to let Stanley, their golden retriever pup in.

The pup immediately tumbled over himself in his enthusiasm. Frank gave him a long rub as he snuffed and chuffed. When the youngest member of the family settled down, Frank fed him.

What Wendy Wants

With Stanley happily crunching away on puppy chow, he got out a pan and put some bacon on to cook.

Frank and Wendy both tried to be healthy eaters, but they allowed themselves bacon and eggs once or twice a week.

By the time Wendy came down in her bathrobe and slippers, Frank had breakfast ready. He smiled at her and pulled out a seat, gesturing grandly, *"Mademoiselle?"*

"Oh, merci, monsieur," she said, tucking her bathrobe under her as she sat, as if it were an expensive dress. Wendy poured the orange juice.

"This looks yummy," she said.

Sitting across from her, he met her gaze and said, "So do you."

Her eyes bright with happiness, she laughed. "Thank you.'

"What did your sister say?"

"I hope you don't mind. She and Samuel are having a few friends over for a BBQ lunch, the usual suspects, Jack and Madeline, Terry and Janice, and Rick and Mary are coming. She wants us to have lunch when we pick up the boys. I said yes, I hope that's okay."

"Sure, sounds like fun."

What Wendy Wants

They discussed then, about how easy it had been for them to slip into a kind of comfy 'marital melancholy.'

Wendy expelled a deep breath. "I just don't know how it happened."

He shook his head. "You are the most important person in my life – other than our kids, of course. I'm so proud of you for telling me everything you did. We haven't been honest with each other. I've been reading that André Chevalier character. You know the Frenchman in all those stories?"

Wendy giggled. Mentioning the French Dom instantly lightened the conversation. "I love André," she confessed.

"What's not to love about André?" he agreed. "Anyway, he says that, *'Deceit is a barrier to intimacy,'* and I have to agree. We've been lying to each other and it's created walls around ourselves. Somehow we've slowly been drifting apart. I don't want that to happen to us. What we have together is far too important."

"I agree," she said. "But how have *you* been deceitful?"

"Sweetheart, I masturbate every single day, sometimes twice a day."

Her eyes widened. "Seriously? But why?"

He shrugged. "I didn't want to always be coming on to you, you know? I sometimes feel as though you're normal and I'm a sex fiend. Besides, you haven't been that interested in making love and now I know why. I'm not satisfying you."

"Oh, Frank, I'm really sorry."

"Don't be. We're both to blame." He shook his head. "When I saw the books you were reading... it blew me away. I realized then that you think about sex *a lot*."

He raised his eyebrows up and down wickedly and gave her a naughty grin. "Maybe even as much as I do. You have a vibrator and you masturbate without me, too."

She looked a little sheepish at that. "That's true."

He touched her on the hand. "It's a good thing, sweetheart."

Wendy's lips quirked up in a relieved smile. "I'm so glad that we're talking about this. I've tried to give you hints, honey, I wish I'd had the guts to come out and say it. I don't know why this subject is so difficult to talk about. It's embarrassing to try to explain to you what I want."

His brows drew down in a frown.

She shrugged her hair back and rolled her eyes in a depreciating manner. "Especially when I'm still figuring out what I like myself."

What Wendy Wants

"It doesn't matter." He smiled. "We'll have fun trying *everything*. I'm going to work hard to keep the woman I love happy. Together, we're going to discover each other's fantasies and act every one of them out. But I don't think we have time for anything else this morning."

Her lips curved up at that, but when she checked the time she frowned.

"Crap, it's late. I told Dawn I'd bring a potato bake, too. We've got to get ready to go."

Frank gave her an exaggerated sigh. "That's too bad. We'll have to try out the blindfold and handcuffs I bought later."

Wendy's startled expression, closely followed by her exuberant laugh made him laugh, too.

What Wendy Wants

BBQ

Frank

~~~

Stanley snuffed and skipped excitedly, playfully holding his leash in his mouth. He loved riding in the car. Actually, the little pup loved doing anything with his family.

Frank lifted him into the dog cage in the back of Wendy's SUV, gave him one last pat and shut the car door.

The drive to the Morrow's home was short. The high altitude and customary deep blue sky made for another beautiful day in Colorado.

Wendy's sister, Dawn and her husband, Samuel Morrow, lived on Cheyenne Mountain Boulevard in a five bedroom home. They had a heated pool with a spiral children's slide, hot tub, trampoline and a clubhouse for their girls. Frank figured that a small family could easily and comfortably reside in that clubhouse.

Wendy and Frank's three boys – Will, Anthony and Jeff – loved to visit the Morrows because there was so much to do at their house. Samuel's family was very successful in banking and as the oldest son, Samuel was, too.

What Wendy Wants

The home they lived in cost a fortune, as Samuel constantly reminded anyone who would listen.

As usual, the Morrow's BBQ event was something like a circus. Five couples and their children attended, two dogs and enough food for a hundred spread out on two patio tables as an all-you-can-eat buffet.

After the cooking was finished, the outdoor BBQ area was turned into a small camp-style fire that provided a 'camp ground' feeling for the nippy afternoon atmosphere.

No matter what was happening, Frank's gaze returned again and again to Wendy. He was drawn to her. Just like the needle of a compass changes position, continually seeking north; Wendy was Frank's 'true north.'

Her eyes continually moved to him, as well.

As if they shared some sort of strong, psychic connection, he always knew *exactly* where she was. Each time their eyes met, it felt as if they were reading each other's minds.

Happiness, unity and sensual pleasures remembered and shared were telegraphed between them.

Their day was filled with shy blushes, goofy, knowing smiles and raised eyebrows.

What Wendy Wants

Frank felt like a newlywed on his honeymoon.

Was this what one night of seduction could do? Wow. He was impressed. He'd never expected to experience that indescribable rush of 'new love' again – not after all this time as a married man.

What he felt toward Wendy was even better than new love. It was mature, time - tested *true love* that had been revitalized. They'd both realized what they had and what they could have lost.

Their marriage was only going to get better from here on out.

Later, the women went inside while he and the other men stayed out near the fire, watching the children play, drinking a nice smooth Merlot and chatting.

"Man, I'm so sick of this *'Fifty shades of bullshit'* crap that's going around," Rick said. A local Real Estate broker; his wife was pregnant with her second child. "The movie's coming out, too. That's only going to only add to the madness."

"What? Is Mary into that porno horseshit, too?" Samuel asked.

"You know it."

Rick shook his head in the typical male, baffled expression of disbelief. "Women," he mocked. "It's Christian Grey this, Christian

What Wendy Wants

Grey that. Why don't *you* read it, honey? You'd like it," he said, mimicking a high-pitched female voice.

The men laughed, but Frank remained silent.

Frank's naturally curious and analytical mind stirred. What was going on here?

These guys didn't have a clue. They were spending their energy spouting off about something that they obviously knew nothing about. And to criticize their wives based on totally uninformed, close-minded ignorance?

In Frank's opinion that pretty much defined stupidity.

"Is Dawn trying to get you to read that book, too?" Jack asked.

Jack, the youngest of their group, was Vice Principle of the local High School. He'd been married six years. They hadn't started a family yet as they were intentionally waiting until they were in a better financial position.

"There's no way I'd read that stupid porn," Samuel scoffed. "I can't believe that a mature, intelligent woman would be interested in that crap."

"C'mon Samuel," Frank had to respond to that comment. "Are you telling me that you've never watched a bit of internet porn?"

What Wendy Wants

The man had the good grace to become red-faced. "Of course I have," he admitted. "I'm a man, after all. I see a little bit from time to time, the operative word being a 'little bit.' But I don't waste all my valuable time on it. These women read these books, join book clubs and spend every minute reading this time-wasting smut."

The whole conversation was a real eye-opener for Frank.

His friends were a bunch of idiots.

Isolated by his highly enjoyable forensic accounting puzzles, Frank hadn't even *noticed* what Wendy had been reading. That made him an idiot, too.

Lucky for him, the neglect of his wife was a flaw that he'd become aware of and now knew how to mend.

At least these guys had known their wives' interests. But why were they all so close-minded and judgmental?

The conversation went on, with every man except Frank joining in. Each one of them criticized their spouses for 'wasting time' with their 'poor taste' in reading material – without even reading it themselves to know what they were criticizing!

It astonished Frank. Complaints like, 'All she does is read smut,' and 'Her IQ is probably dropping several points with every book,' were common.

What Wendy Wants

Finally, Frank couldn't listen to one more word. He'd never been more ashamed of the male gender. What a bunch of mocking, cynical, sanctimonious hypocrites! They were incredibly stupid, too.

Talk about shooting themselves in the foot. *Or an even more precious body part*, he thought wryly.

He knew that if he said anything he'd be sticking his neck out for a whole load of ridicule. Yet he didn't want them to think that because he didn't say anything that he'd agreed with them.

"I've read it," Frank finally admitted.

"What?" His friends answered practically in unison.

They all turned to look at him as if he'd just grown antlers – or perhaps as if he'd admitted dressing in women's clothes.

The instant Frank had opened Wendy's Kindle, he knew that he wasn't sexually satisfying Wendy. It was so obvious.

Why were these guys missing the implications of their partners reading erotic fiction?

This was about *sex*, something that pricked the ears – (and other parts!) – of all men everywhere.

Yet not one of them considered that their wives were getting hot and bothered while reading.

What Wendy Wants

Erotic romance was *foreplay* for a woman.

These guys could use that to improve their own marriages. Hell, they could read a book *with* their partner to get them in the mood.

Here were four generally intelligent men, blinded by what? A refusal to try something new? Or was it some sort of natural prejudice?

What a waste of a golden opportunity. Frank had noticed that he'd felt jealous of his wife's book boyfriends.

Was that what it was? Were these guys putting their partners down as a way to stroke their own egos?

If so, maybe it was pride that was blinding them because their masculinity was being threatened.

"I've read *Fifty Shades*," he said calmly. "So far, I've only skimmed parts of it, really, but it's one of the books that I plan to read."

"Why would you do that?" Samuel demanded. He looked insulted, as if Frank's admission was a personal attack on him.

"Why wouldn't I?"

He was met with more blank, confused stares.

Frank reflected on Wendy's Kindle and some of her highlighted notes that she'd made from that book.

What Wendy Wants

"The parts that I read were hot. Besides, my wife is interested in it and I'm interested in anything that's important to her."

Somehow, his speech had silenced every man there. No one knew what to say, but Frank did.

"I wonder if women read smut because they aren't being satisfied?" he idly suggested. "It could be that many women get bored with sex. Maybe they'd like to mix things up from time to time and try something new."

He had every man's attention as they all stared at him wide-eyed.

A long moment passed.

Could he make them think? If his friends tried opening up their minds, perhaps they could be rewarded with some amazingly hot sex. Maybe they could revitalize their marriages, too.

Frank raised his wine glass in salute. "I've read my wife's smut and not only do I enjoy it, but I've also learned things."

Recalling last night, he gave them a wicked, self-satisfied smile. "I've learned *a lot* of things, actually. And do you know what else? Ever since I started reading Wendy's erotic novels, I've never had so much mind-blowing sex in my life."

There was another stunned silence.

What Wendy Wants

Jack, always the wise guy of the group said, "Wow, if your wife Wendy finds out about that, you're a dead man!"

That broke the tension and got a laugh all around, but Frank noticed the others still glanced at him with uncertainty, curiosity and strangely, respect, for the rest of the evening.

Epilogue

Wendy sat in her bedroom and looked at the clock. It was almost 10pm.

The kids were settled. Jeff, their youngest was fast asleep. The twins had been threatened with pain of death if they dared to disturb her.

The twins weren't stupid.

Wendy figured that they knew that their mom and dad enjoyed their love life. The twins probably even figured out that she and their father enjoyed cyber-sex whenever he was away.

While family was important, the twins were starting to realize that their mom and dad had a separate married life, too. How could that harm them?

Wendy hoped when their children married that they would each have an honest, satisfying love life of their own.

Wendy had ten more minutes to get ready. Ten minutes to utterly banish 'mom brain' and get sexy, slutty, 'wife brain' into gear.

No sweat.

What Wendy Wants

The last few weeks with Frank had been amazing. Nothing was forbidden.

They'd enjoyed shower and bathtub sex and made love all over their bedroom. He'd taken her over the couch, against the wall and on the stairs.

Wendy adored bondage and even being blindfolded. Naughty words and authoritative commands also buzzed her.

Frank it turned out, loved anything that she loved.

That was good because he had a few hidden fantasies of his own that she enjoyed.

She got under the covers, the sheets brushing against her sensitive nipples. The little bag of toys Frank had given her was in a pillowcase beside her.

What had he been up to? He was a bad, bad man. No doubt he'd left something really wicked in there to surprise her.

Wendy had a surprise or two of her own.

Frank was on a business trip in Bridgeport, Connecticut, for the next four days. However, for months now, they had been playing cyber-sex games whenever Frank had to travel for work.

What Wendy Wants

Who would have thought that her love life could be so much fun? Or that she could have so many orgasms?

'Use it or you lose it' was a saying that applied in this case. That and *'Practice makes perfect.'*

Wendy figured that her husband had trained her body so well that she could almost climax on his command.

When she was first married, Wendy thought of Frank at all times. Love was a chemistry that caused constant, overwhelming euphoria. It was a feeling that mesmerized and commanded all her thoughts and attention.

Frank became her focus.

Wendy adored getting dressed up for him, shaving and creaming her skin to make it soft for his enjoyment. She'd taken such care with her appearance.

Then all of that just… went away.

How had they let their together time of making love – such a fun and important part of married life – fall so low in priority?

All that thrill and excitement had eroded so subtly that neither of them had noticed.

What Wendy Wants

Thank God that they had it back again, even better than before. Frank was the father of her children and still her best friend.

Wendy loved him to bits.

The chemistry had become lost for a while, but it had never really gone away.

Now they had no secrets. Wendy and Frank knew each other's every fantasy. They had this wonderful new sexual aspect to their life.

André Chevalier had said, **"Without honest communication there is death to love."**

Frank knew everything, all of her crazy desires and her nasty, naughty thoughts. Wendy had no regrets. She knew what he wanted, too.

Giggling, she imagined them both playing sex games well into their eighties. Lord have mercy, but why not?

Pulling her laptop closer, she stacked up some pillows against the headboard, pulled the sheet up over her and got comfortable.

Frank would be annoyed the moment he saw that sheet covering her body.

He wanted her naked.

What Wendy Wants

She smiled then, thinking of what was under the sheet. Imagining his reaction to her surprise.

It was so incredibly *freeing* being in bed with her husband. She never had to think, or guess what he wanted. She just did whatever he said and *yum*. The things he had her do!

He made her climax again and again and again, much more than she ever did when she was younger.

A chime signaled that Frank was on the other line. What would her devious husband come up with tonight?

With a thrill of excitement she hit answer.

Frank's smiling, handsome face came on the screen and her hand immediately when to her throat.

The rough look of him with laugh lines around his mouth and slight creases at the corners of his eyes made something in her chest tighten with adoration, raw passion and love.

Big, tough, commanding and demanding. He was so incredibly attractive.

Men. Someday, when Frank's hair went grey, he would still look handsome and distinguished, *the rat*.

What Wendy Wants

It always seemed to her that men just got hotter while women looked *old*.

Frank regularly told her that she was the most beautiful woman in the world.

Grinning, she considered that her husband was a charming suck-up. Please Lord, may he never change.

His hotel room must have been warm because Frank was shirtless, wearing only blue jeans. She delighted in the clean line of his jaw and his smooth muscular chest.

How lucky was she to have married such a sexy guy? He was big and masculine and he'd discovered the sensual thrill of dominating her. Hell, not just discovered — it was more like he'd fully embraced the concept, jumping right in and running the show.

Talk about stimulus and response.

Just the thought of Frank made her wet.

When he saw her, he frowned. His eyebrows rose and he gave her a stern look.

"Why is my wife covered in a sheet? You know that I like to see you naked."

What Wendy Wants

Wendy smirked. "Well, it's because I have a surprise for my handsome husband."

"Do you?" Frank sat forward, his eyes glinting with interest.

She licked her lips and nodded.

"You haven't looked into the bag I left for you have you?"

"Nope."

"Good. Are you ready to follow my commands?" he asked, slipping into that stern domineering tone he used when he ordered her around sexually. Frank's voice was deep anyway, but when he was turned on it went even lower, with a husky, lust-filled overtone.

"Oh yes, Sir," she said with a grin.

"Who does your body belong to?"

"You, Sir," she giggled.

"That's right," he growled. "And you're a very bad girl for covering yourself. I suspect that I'll need to spank you when I get home. Take those sheets off. I want to see my wife naked, you gorgeous, slutty little sex toy, you."

Wendy sat up and pulled her covers off. Focusing the camera on her pubic area, she was hyperaware of Frank's quick intake of breath.

What Wendy Wants

The look on his face was perfect. Wendy could swear that she saw his brown eyes, already dark with lust, darken further.

Frank clearly loved her surprise.

"Goddamn it, Wendy that's the hottest thing I've ever seen," he growled.

Wendy had given herself a French wax – waxing her pubic area while leaving a narrow vertical strip in front which ended just before her clitoris. Her labia was utterly bare, her already aroused clitoris poking out.

Wendy had to laugh. The pleasure at his words made her face ache, her grin was so large.

"I really hoped you'd liked it, Sir."

"Like it? I can't wait to get back from this trip so I can explore every clean shaven inch of that sweet little cunt of yours with my tongue. Clever girl. I don't think I would've thought of it."

Frank unzipped himself, lowering his jeans while drawing his heavy erection out. He circled it with his palm and fingers and began to pull himself with long, slow strokes.

What Wendy Wants

Wendy was entranced. The erotic sight of her husband working his thickly veined cock made her temperature rise. Without thinking, she moved her hand lower, between her legs to touch herself.

"Wendy," Frank said sternly.

She pulled her hand back as if her aching pussy had burnt her. Her eyes flew to his face at that deceptively mild tone.

"Did I give you permission to touch yourself?"

"No, Sir," she admitted, chagrined. "Sorry, Sir."

"I'll punish you later," he told her.

The sensual menace in his tone made her internal muscles clench. They both loved his 'punishments.' Discipline was all part of their sex games and man, she sure came hard no matter what he did. Nothing made her hotter than him taking control and putting his hands all over her.

Frank knew exactly how turned-on she was. Studying her with an avid, hungry expression he said, "Get the bag out."

"Oh, yes, Sir," Wendy said breathlessly and did so.

Wendy took out the bag he'd left her, delighted by the no-nonsense, yet turned-on look on Frank's face.

What Wendy Wants

"Do you see the new nipple clamps I got you? They're right at the top in large clear wrapping."

Wendy frowned as she looked through the bag and pulled out the envelope. She already owned tweezer clamps. These new ones had a metal chain linking them. A screw could tighten or loosen each clamp.

"Hold your breasts out to me and pull on those sweet nipples. I want to see them pucker, becoming hard and ready."

She did so until they protruded, sharp enough to cut glass.

"Good girl," he praised. "I wish I was there to run my tongue over them."

Wendy moaned at the thought and he laughed.

"You're such a beautiful, needy little slut. I'm going to make you come for hours tonight. Now put those clamps on."

Wendy's hands trembled with adrenaline and lust as she did. Frank directed her and watched intently while she placed them. They were tighter than the other ones. The weight of the chain pulled, increasing sensation.

Wendy knew she was already wet and ready. The pinching bite of the clamps made her groan.

"How do they feel?"

What Wendy Wants

"Hot," she said with instant, open candor. She kept no sexual secrets from her husband, not anymore. "They're a turn on, for sure. The aching sensation on my nipples seems to shoot straight to my crotch."

Frank smiled. "Good. They look fantastic. Your nipples are going to be sore the whole time I'm away. I want you constantly reminded of how hard I intend to use you when I get back."

These erotic words made her whimper. Jesus, Frank was turning her into a total nymphomaniac.

"Get the vibrator out, the Lelo."

Wendy was very glad to do so. They had a Hitachi, but Wendy found it too strong for her needs.

Lelo was a Swedish company and her newest vibrator was a waterproof 'rabbit' device. One part went inside, cleverly massaging her G spot; the other stimulated her clitoris.

Wendy liked it because it had a handle and Frank could fuck her with it, or she could fuck herself while he watched.

They'd also bought remote-controlled pleasure beads that rotated and vibrated at the same time. They were made to be worn discreetly inside. The top beads rotated against her G-spot, while the lower beads delivered powerful vibrations. Every setting was adjustable via wireless remote.

Frank took her to a restaurant while wearing those beads – wicked, teasing tormentor that he was.

Talk about practicing orgasm control.

What a change. Once it had been really difficult to get herself off.

Now she had to fight not to.

Frank had forbidden her to have a climax without him. Every single day she seemed to always be a bit on the boil, just waiting for the opportunity.

"Turn it to the lowest setting and insert it," he ordered, still working his thick shaft with his hand. It was so sexy to watch Frank stroke his big cock. It made her mouth water.

"Yes, Sir," she breathed, doing as he said.

"Good girl. Now spread those thighs for me and make sure the camera is in the right position. I want to watch your cunt drip and tighten as you come."

"Oh, God," she gasped as she did as he directed.

What Wendy Wants

"Yeah, baby, you are so fucking hot for it, aren't you?" he asked gruffly, fisting himself faster.

His enormous erection was deep red, almost purple. It was also damp with pre-cum, his balls heavy with need.

"*You* make me hot for it, Sir."

Wendy loved the effect she had on him. Seeing how hard she made him only added to her heady sense of pleasure. Frank *craved* her. He made her feel desirable and beautiful.

"Squeeze your breasts and lay down now," he said. "Turn the vibrator on to pulse, I know you love that. It's hard for you *not* to come when the vibrator is on pulse. I want to see you thrust those hips up as you climax. I want you to imagine my big cock is pounding deep inside you."

Wendy put the vibrator on pulse and continued squeezing her breasts. Her nipples pressed tightly in the clamps, radiated sensation right down to her sex. All the while she heard herself making soft sounds of need and erotic pleasure.

Adding to it all was the knowledge that her husband watched closely while the vibrator did its job.

What Wendy Wants

That familiar tight coiling of need gripped low in her stomach and pelvic area. She was panting now, and her pulse pounded in her ears and throat.

Breathless and writhing, Wendy moaned.

"You know what I'm going to do to you when I get home?" he asked in a low, seductive voice. "I'm going to take you doggy style on your hands and knees. Your head will be down, with your ass right up in the air. It's going to be pink from a spanking. I love taking you, fucking you *hard* from behind."

"Oh, God, please…"

"I'm going to eat that sweet cunt of yours out, too."

"Please, Frank, please," Wendy begged.

"Please, what?"

"Please let me come, Sir!"

"You can't wait?"

"No, no," she cried out as raw need flowed through her. "I have to, Frank. Please. Please let me."

Wendy wanted him to watch, wanted him to witness how easily he could make her orgasm.

What Wendy Wants

With her pussy shaved bare, she was completely exposed. Frank would see it all. She knew that with her husband's curious carnal mind, her climax would only make him harder.

"Go ahead then, go over, baby. Let me see it," he growled.

Her whole body trembled with molten heat at the command.

"That's right baby," he said in a deep guttural voice. "Come for me."

"Ah, ah, ah… Frank," she cried out.

Her heels pushed down into the bed as Wendy thrust upwards, arching her hips in a convulsion of pure ecstasy.

Her husband, jerking himself off, grunted loudly and then he groaned.

The erotic sounds and awareness of his climax heightened her orgasm. It sent a blast of pleasure through her, body heart and soul. Frank had found his own release at virtually the same moment as her climax.

Coming exactly at the same time was common for them now.

Wendy hit the remote to turn the vibrator off. She lay for a long while, panting and catching her breath. Boneless and mindless, she languidly drifted in a sated happy state.

What Wendy Wants

"Better take those clamps off," Frank said. "Jesus, woman, you're going to have to change those sheets you're so damn wet."

Wendy snickered and showed him the folded towel she'd put underneath her.

Frank often told her that when they played Dominance and submission games, Wendy flooded the bed, making much more of a damp spot than he ever did.

It was true, really.

She used the towel to wipe herself and then took the clamps off, rubbing her sore nipples as the blood flowed back.

If Frank were here, he would be soothing them with his mouth and tongue.

Having both reached orgasm, they chatted over the day, smiling at each other in companionable accord.

Eventually Frank told her to look into his bag of tricks again and this time to pull out dildo he'd bought her.

When Wendy found it she cracked up. "Frank!" she squealed, incredulous at the size of the huge phallus. "Just what am I supposed to do with this?"

What Wendy Wants

He raised and lowered his eyebrows suggestively, a naughty little smirk on his face. Wendy loved it when he was playful like this. He was so much *fun*.

"Don't you worry about that," he said. "I have a few things in mind. I'll tell you *exactly* what I want done with it. Keep looking. There's something else in there, too."

She pulled out a smaller phallic object. *Shit*. Her stomach tightened. It looked like an anal plug.

"Really? Are you going where I think you're going here, Sir?"

He had the good grace to look a little sheepish. "Maybe."

It was another thirty minutes before they were both utterly sated and ready to sleep. When they finally finished playing they blew each other kisses good night.

"I love you, honey," she said.

"I love you, too. I'm the luckiest guy in the world, Wendy."

"Back at cha, baby," she replied. "Only I am the luckiest girl."

Wendy disconnected, slipped on a nightgown and settled into bed with a happy sigh.

What Wendy Wants

Tomorrow she would remember feelings and events from tonight. The ache of a tender nipple or the image of Frank's hooded, dark eyes and firm lips would bring it all back.

Wendy's friends had commented about the sudden, inexplicable smiles she often wore. They had asked her, what had changed? Why was she suddenly so much happier? But how could she explain it to them?

Sex wasn't everything, but it was one very important thing – particularly within a marriage.

Who would have thought that her life could have changed so completely? All because her genius husband had accidentally taken her Kindle to work, had broken into it and was curious and honest and stubborn enough to make her every sexual fantasy come true.

All was right in her world.

She thought of the new erotic romance she'd read and found that she was grinning.

That was the other sneaky surprise that she had in store for Frank while he was away.

Wendy had downloaded it onto his Kindle. Had he been too busy to find it there? Or maybe he'd read it already.

What Wendy Wants

Knowing him, he'd have taken notes. Was he planning to surprise her with some new sex game when he got home?

I just love surprises, she mused happily.

Worn out, with a contented smile on her face, Wendy drifted off.

In her last conscious moments before she fell asleep, she thought of her husband.

Just what, she wondered, was that handsome, clever man of hers going to think of next?

The End

Made in the USA
Lexington, KY
28 December 2017